GW00738277

GIRL
ON THE RUN
BOOK 1
RINGMASTER

ALSO BY JULIA GOLDING

The Diamond of Drury Lane

Cat among the Pigeons

Den of Thieves

Cat O' Nine Tails

Cat's Cradle

Empty Quarter

Secret of the Sirens

The Gorgon's Gaze

Mines of the Minotaur

The Chimera's Curse

The Ship Between the Worlds

JULIA GOLDING

GIRL ON THE RUN

BOOK 1
RINGMASTER

EGMONT

For Dad,

who has the gift of quiet encouragement

EGMONT

We bring stories to life

First published 2007
This edition published 2011 by Egmont UK Ltd
239 Kensington High Street, London W8 6SA

ISBN 978 1 4052 4734 4

1 3 5 7 9 10 8 6 4 2

www.egmont.co.uk
www.juliagolding.co.uk

A CIP catalogue record for this title is available from the British Library

Typeset by Avon DataSet Ltd, Bidford on Avon, Warwickshire
Printed and bound in Great Britain by the CPI Group

Julia Golding

Julia Golding read English at Cambridge then joined the Foreign Office and served in Poland. Her work as a diplomat took her from the high point of town twinning in the Tatra Mountains to the low of inspecting the bottom of a Silesian coal mine.

On leaving Poland, she exchanged diplomacy for academia and took a doctorate in the literature of the English Romantic Period at Oxford. She then joined Oxfam as a lobbyist on conflict issues, campaigning at the UN and with governments to lessen the impact of conflict on civilians living in war zones.

Married with three children, Julia now lives in Oxford. Her first book, *The Diamond of Drury Lane,* won the Nestlé Children's Book Prize and Waterstones' Children's Book Prize, and was shortlisted for the Costa Children's Book Award.

1

07.00, Nairobi, Kenya: Hot and dry, storm approaching.

Looking back, the day had started much like any other. Darcie had resisted her father's attempts to get her up for school – a job delegated to him by Mom when she went to the States to get her regular manicure. Darcie hadn't actually stirred out of bed until the Kenyan maid, Tegla, came in with her ironed shirt and threw open the curtains. The drama of the swift equatorial sunrise had already passed; the sun was beating down on the lawn as the gardener watered the crimson flowers of the hibiscus that rioted on the wall opposite.

'Mr Lock, he say hurry up,' said Tegla hanging the shirt on the wardrobe.

'Mmrumph,' answered Darcie from the depths of her pillow.

Tegla passed the bed and slapped her on the rump as she would one of her own children. 'And I say you are lazy girl. My Winston has been up for hours.'

This didn't make Darcie feel any better. Just at that moment she hated Winston. She hauled herself out of bed and fell into her clothes. Running a quick comb through her black hair, she bunched it back and inspected herself in the mirror. She looked a mess. Darcie grinned, knowing that Mom wasn't here to disapprove of her tomboy of a daughter.

Darcie clattered into the kitchen to find her father sitting with a copy of Kenya's leading daily newspaper propped up on the teapot. A lizard scuttled up the whitewashed wall and disappeared into the rafters. The kitchen smelt of the freshly squeezed passion fruit juice – Darcie's favourite, prepared for her breakfast by Tegla. Mr Lock flicked his eyes up to his daughter, a small frown settling on his face. Mr Lock was immaculate with his crisp shirt and tie, grey suit with jacket hung neatly on the back of his chair, carefully groomed hair and moustache.

'Every morning –'

Here it came – the daily lecture from Mr Grouch.

'– I see Tegla ironing your shirt but by the time you've decided to grace us with your presence, it looks as if it has spent the night at the bottom of the wash basket. How do you do it?' He moved her schoolbag off the chair beside him to make room for her.

'Just a talent of mine, Dad. You're lucky to have such a gifted child,' replied Darcie, grabbing a piece of bread and spreading it with guava jam.

'Well, one thing's sure: you didn't inherit it from your mother or me.' Mr Lock flapped the newspaper over a page and subsided into the sports section.

'Has Mom rung at all?' asked Darcie through a mouthful.

Mr Lock shifted the paper uneasily. 'No, Darcie. You know she doesn't like to call when she's in New York.'

'Gosh, having your nails done must require *so* much concentration,' said Darcie sardonically. She resented her mom being away so often for no very good reason.

'Look, Darcie. She's busy. She'll call when she can.'

Darcie stared at her father's bent head. She prayed she would not end up like him when she got older –

neat, steady, set in her ways, doing some dead-end job in the consular section of the British High Commission. She knew she wouldn't end up like her mother – the only highlight in *her* life being to fly once a month to the States just to file her fingernails and do some serious shopping. Darcie promised herself that she was going to do something much more interesting – be an explorer, play international women's soccer, fence in the Olympics, something exciting, different at the very least.

Her father stood up. 'Hurry or you'll make me miss my first meeting.'

Darcie trailed out of the kitchen, toast in hand, schoolbag dragging on the floor.

'I might be a little late back tonight,' her father announced as he reversed their car out of the garage. The guard waved them off before shutting the blue gates, hiding the secret world of their lush green compound from the dusty road. 'Will you be all right?'

'I'll be fine. You don't have to worry, you know.'

As they drove towards the international school,

Darcie watched the local kids standing at bus stops by the side of the road, all dressed in clean white shirts no matter how poor their background. She wondered how their mothers managed it. Her own rich life so close to so much poverty sometimes seemed wrong.

Michael Lock smiled at his daughter's serious expression. 'I know I shouldn't worry, but it's habit. I trust you not to get up to any mischief in my absence.'

'Do I ever?'

'No. You're not a bad kid for a grumpy old man like me.' He tooted as a male cyclist wobbled in front of him out of a side road, a woman sitting on the back and a live chicken strapped to the handlebars.

'You're not old!' protested Darcie.

'But you think I'm grumpy?'

She met his eye and grinned.

'It's my age, Darcie. Miserable midlife hormones – I can't help it.'

'Hey, hang on!' Darcie cried in mock outrage. 'I'm the teenager here. I'm the one who's supposed to have the raging hormones!'

Michael Lock pulled up outside the school gate.

'No wonder your mom needs a break from us both once a month. Here, don't forget your bag!'

School had passed in the usual blur of lessons and time misspent kicking a ball about with some boys under the mango tree during breaks. In the heat of the day, she'd cooled off in the school pool playing water polo, and then dozed through the next classes.

After the final bell, Darcie took a taxi to her fencing lesson at the Country Club. She didn't have any real friends at school at the moment: the transient life of the international community meant that no sooner had she formed one attachment than it was ripped up as her family moved on. It worried her that she didn't seem to fit in unless as part of the short-lived camaraderie of a sports team. The guys just looked at her as an honorary boy with a mean right foot. With the girls she struggled to keep up with their interests of clothes and boyfriends, frankly finding both subjects boring. They'd long ago sensed she was an outsider so rarely included her in their social life. So the club was where she preferred to hang out after classes as she could be part of something without feeling lonely. You could ride, play tennis, polo, learn almost any sport there.

The defence attaché at the High Commission had taken up her dad's challenge to teach his daughter a 'civilised sport rather than all that ball-kicking nonsense'. Major Parker had been British fencing champion in his youth and brought to the lessons an uncompromising standard. Today he had been particularly testy, picking holes in her technique until she felt like hurling both abuse and her gauntlets at his shiny red face. She bit her tongue instead. Good fencers never lost their temper and she was determined to be the best.

It wasn't until after the major dropped her at the corner of her road that she suspected something was wrong. The gates to the bungalow stood wide open. Darcie rushed into the house, making her way to the kitchen at the back. Tegla was nowhere to be seen, no supper had been prepared. She peeked out the window. Winston was not waiting on the lawn to play football as he usually did. Most worrying was the disappearance of the guard at the compound gate. And Zorro? Where was the black Alsatian? Darcie dumped her schoolbag and raced around the garden. Nothing and nobody. Just a chain with an empty collar by the open front gate.

Darcie was scared: Nairobi was notorious for violent burglaries and the absence of the Kenyan staff was ominous. She tried not to panic. First things first. She closed the gate. Now, the telephone – she'd ring the High Commission. Dad was probably still working late.

'Hello, British High Commission,' said the lady on the switchboard. 'How may I help you?'

'Can I speak to Michael Lock please?'

There was a pause.

'Michael Lock,' repeated the lady.

'Yes, Michael Lock. Consular section.'

Another pause.

'I'm afraid we no longer have a Mr Lock in our

consular section,' the lady replied. 'Can I put you through to someone else?'

'No,' snapped Darcie. 'Look, I know he works there.'

'I'm sorry but Michael Lock is not on our staff.'

Darcie pummelled the sofa cushion in frustration. She knew that voice. It was the old lady who sat sometimes at reception. She'd even met her at Christmas parties. She dredged through her memory to see if she could think of her name.

'It's Mrs Smith, isn't it – Gladys Smith?'

Silence.

'Mrs Smith, it's me, it's Darcie. Dad's not come home and there's no one here. I'm worried. I need to talk to someone.'

Darcie thought she could hear clicking and shuffling on the other end of the phone.

'Sit tight, Darcie. Someone's coming for you,' said the woman – and put the phone down.

That wasn't good enough. Darcie wasn't about to sit tight in an empty house. If the High Commission were going to be so useless, she'd call someone else. Darcie leafed through the family address book. It had very few entries, her parents having a small circle of acquaintances and no relatives. There seemed nothing for it but to call her mom's friend, Doreen Clutterbuck. A blonde Texan with silver-painted nails, Darcie couldn't bear her normally but this was an emergency. She rifled through to the right page and picked up the phone.

Beeeep.

The line sounded funny – it wasn't dialling. Then nothing. Not the faintest whirring or click of the Kenyan telephone exchange.

Darcie swore and slammed the phone down. Why hadn't her stupid parents given her a mobile like she'd asked them? If they'd listened to her, she wouldn't be stuck now. But what did the dead line mean? Was there a problem at the telephone exchange? Or had some housebreakers lured the staff away and now cut off the phone, leaving a fourteen-year-old girl alone to defend her home?

But what about Gladys Smith and her claim Michael

Lock didn't work at the consulate any more? Darcie rubbed her eyes. She didn't have time to think about that. It was all too weird.

She went to the window looking out on the driveway. Were the thieves going to break in now they'd cut the phones off? She couldn't see anyone. The sun was sinking behind the palm trees fringing the road to the city centre. The air was sour with the smell of rubbish and wood fires from the street corner. In the distance she could hear the call to prayer crackling on the loudspeaker from the mosque. Everyone else was going about their normal business – shopping, cooking, travelling home. No one had noticed that Blue Gates Bungalow had abruptly dropped out of normality.

Should she sit tight or go looking for help?

Mrs Smith had told her to wait – but then she had said Michael Lock no longer worked there, which was obviously wrong.

She'd also said someone would come for her. Darcie decided to give it a few minutes. They must realise this was an emergency. Someone would be round from the High Commission very soon to explain.

Darcie sat on the veranda and hugged her knees, a torch and the gardener's spade for protection. A mosquito whined in her ear. She slapped it away. The night-time chorus of cicadas swung into action, finding a pitch just within human hearing, shrill enough to grate on the eardrum like thousands of squeaky hinges. It was hot.

Darcie waited.

And waited.

Soon it was too late to go and search for help from one of the neighbours. She might get shot at if she turned up unannounced at one of the well-fortified mansions that surrounded her family's modest bungalow. People round here were edgy since the most recent spate of burglaries. Someone would come for her.

At midnight, a black car with diplomatic plates turned up at the gate and switched off its lights. A moment later, two men got out. And that was when the madness began.

2

The two dark-suited men sat in the kitchen, watching her closely. Darcie looked down at her scuffed trainers waiting for them to say something. But since asking to come in, they had not spoken. She had to break the silence.

'Where is everyone?'

The taller of the pair – the one with the American accent – glanced at his British counterpart with a look that said 'Go on, you tell her.' The Brit, a fat man with balding hair and an east London accent, shook his head slightly, refusing the task.

Darcie bunched her fists, knuckles white on the gleaming tabletop.

'Will you just tell me what's going on?'

'We don't know,' the Brit finally admitted.

'What d'you mean, you don't know?'

'Exactly that. Your dad's disappeared.'

Darcie refused to believe him. 'But my dad can't

disappear! He left here for the High Commission this morning. He can't have just vanished!'

The American frowned, drumming his fingers on the table. Darcie felt furious as well as scared; why weren't they helping her? Why did she have to force every bit of information out of them?

'What about Mom? Does she know?'

'Your mom's fine,' said the American quickly. 'She's just had to go to ground for a while – until this is sorted.'

The Brit turned to his colleague. 'What do you think?'

Now they were talking over her head. If this carried on any longer she was going to throw something at them. The jam pot – that would do. She prided herself on being as good a shot as Winston, or any of the guys on the school baseball team.

'Your call, my friend. She's one of yours.'

'Well, actually, she's also yours. Got dual nationality.'

'But you'll take care of her? Isn't that what we agreed?'

'Yes.'

'Look!' shouted Darcie, jumping to her feet, fist now curled round the cool glass of the jam jar like a hand grenade. 'Either you tell me what's going on or you get the hell out of here!'

The men looked at each other.

'She'll do,' said the American.

The Brit stepped forward and put a hand on Darcie's shoulder to make her sit down again.

'Calm down, we're going to tell you. But first you've got to agree that when we leave, this conversation never happened.'

'Wh . . . what?'

'It never happened.'

Darcie shrugged. This was daft but what did that matter if she was finally going to get some answers?

'What I'm about to tell you must never be repeated to anyone, understood?'

Darcie nodded.

'I know you think that your dad works at the consulate stamping passports, but you're wrong. He works for us.'

'Us?'

'Come on, Darcie, work it out. The spooks, the

friends, the spies. You've been an embassy kid all your life – surely you know about us?'

Darcie nodded again. Of course, she'd heard about spies working for the Secret Intelligence Services, what the press liked to call MI6, but most of her information had been gathered from watching James Bond films, not from her parents. Occasionally she'd met people from the High Commission who seemed strangely vague about what they did, but never her father. He could describe a visa application in great and boring detail. He had nothing to do with this kind of stuff, surely?

'As for Mrs Lock . . . well, I'll let Agent Eagle here explain.'

'Your mom works for the CIA,' said the American, helping himself to a handful of peanuts on the kitchen counter and cracking them from their shells in his fist.

Darcie shook her head. Hair had escaped from its band and was tickling the back of her neck. She pushed it away irritably. 'No, she doesn't. She's just Mom.' This wasn't even funny.

'Haven't you ever wondered why your mom goes to the States once a month?' interrupted Agent Eagle.

'Nails – to have her nails done.'

'No, Darcie. She goes for her debrief in Washington. She's been running some agents infiltrating a smuggling ring here in Nairobi – making great progress – got us loads of info, until we had to pull her out.'

This was dumb. Her mom working for the CIA – if this was a joke, she wasn't laughing. But then Darcie had never been close to her mother; could she have missed something as big as this? Their relationship had always been cool – hugs and kisses doled out sparingly, no mother-and-daughter sessions to gossip and swap secrets. The distance had grown as Darcie got old enough to despise her mother's lifestyle. Mom had never appeared to want to do anything with her life but play tennis and go to parties. But here was this man suggesting she had been doing more – much, much more.

'And Dad?' croaked Darcie.

'Same. It's a transatlantic operation. He's her

partner. They're the best.' Agent Eagle threw the peanut shells in the bin. 'Or they were until today. Something went wrong. He's gone missing.'

'What are you doing about it? Where is he?'

The Brit took over. It was like watching a relay race as they passed the baton of conversation between them.

'No idea – and we can't do anything for him. You see, his was a deniable operation.'

'A what?'

'He wasn't declared as an intelligence agent to the Kenyan authorities so SIS officially has no knowledge of his clandestine visa dealings – he's on his own.'

'And your mom's had to go underground because if his cover's blown, it probably means hers is too,' added Agent Eagle.

Darcie felt as if she'd wandered into some bizarre Alice-in-Wonderland world where all her certainties had become absurdities. Neat, boring Dad – a British spy. Mom – infiltrating dangerous gangs armed only with her Prada shopping bags. Her parents had been playing with fire. A cold knot of fear tightened in Darcie's chest.

'But what about me?'

'To be honest with you, Darcie, you're a pain in the butt,' said Agent Eagle. 'You shouldn't exist. Agents aren't supposed to have kids together.'

'But listen. The fact is you do exist,' said the Brit in a more kindly tone. 'And this gives us a chance to do something for your father. He's a good man. He knew the risks but he went ahead anyway. He was close to blowing that smuggling circle open – very close.'

Darcie shivered: her dad exposing criminals. Did they think he was already dead? Please someone tell her this was all an elaborate April Fool? Problem was: it was June.

'He was posing as a corrupt consular official, selling passports for dollars, and had wormed his way deep into the traffickers' ring.'

'Traffickers?'

'Yeah, they smuggle people. Drugs. Guns. You name it, they do it.'

'They arm terrorists, run heroin, transport illegals in

the backs of lorries – it's all just a day's work to them,' chipped in Agent Eagle.

'But what difference do I make?' asked Darcie bleakly.

'We can't do anything – but someone in my organisation thinks *you* can,' said the Brit. 'No one will suspect a kid asking questions about her dad. If you agree to join us, acting as a kind of agent, we'll give you all the information we have. That should lead you to the people that have done this to your father. If you get us that far, we can call in some very discreet people to do the rest.'

'The rest?'

'Rescue him, I hope.'

'Splat the bugs – destroy the ring,' added Agent Eagle with an evil grin.

'Can I speak to Mom at least?' Darcie asked. She hugged herself, shivering despite the humid evening.

The American shook his head. 'Not until you leave the country as it might compromise your cover. The people we're up against are as sophisticated as they come – they have all the kit to tap phones if they want and they're bound to be monitoring your family. But you can leave any time, you know. It's your call.'

Leave and be with Mom knowing that she hadn't stayed to help Dad. She couldn't do it.

A dog barked in the night, setting off a chain reaction of howling from all the other compounds. Their serenade was joined by a blast of pop music from a passing taxi. A large grey moth battered itself against the insect screen on the barred windows.

'Just tell me what I've got to do.'

'Come with us now,' said the Brit. 'You can't stay here in any case: we're wrapping up this bit of the operation. You'd better get your things.'

Darcie retreated into her bedroom, hating these two men for doing this to her. She sat on the bed, staring at the Chelsea poster on the wall. Her parents were work colleagues. Agents weren't supposed to have kids together. Was their marriage all a sham too? Playing at parents a game to them? Was she just a useful bit of detail to give their cover more credibility? The only people who could answer these questions were not around to tell her. If she wanted to speak to them again, she'd better get a move on.

Darcie opened her wardrobe and stepped back in shock. It was empty, apart from a small case already full of clothes. So they had known she'd help. They'd already packed her stuff. The whole thing of asking her had been a charade.

3

The two agents left her to check into a room at the Stanley Hotel. A tall security guard stood in the corridor outside, a long black truncheon hanging at his hip. Darcie closed the door and leant against it, dazed as if she had just been hit over the head with the guard's baton, though it had been nothing as physical as that – the blow had been words, just words, spoken in the kitchen by a couple of strangers.

Darcie pushed herself off the door and put the case on the spare bed. Long white net curtains swayed in front of the open window like ghostly brides drifting up the aisle. The street outside was quiet. The air smelt stale as it always did in central Nairobi, still full of the diesel fumes churned out on the traffic-choked streets during daylight hours. It was now three in the morning, a time when the streets belonged to the homeless sleeping in doorways, scavengers rooting through the refuse of the rich, and the mangy cat that bounded across the wall from the hotel dustbins, fishtail dangling from its mouth. There seemed little she could do but undress and lay down on the bed. That was as far as it went. Sleep was impossible. She spent the remainder of the night re-running the memories of her life so far, particularly the last few months, to see if there were any clues that she had missed, something that should have prepared her for the events of the day. She couldn't find anything. Her parents must be good at what they did if even their own child had not suspected them.

She wondered what her mother would be feeling now, stuck somewhere in the States presumably. Had there really been no way to contact her? And Dad? Darcie refused to believe that he was dead. Dad had to be alive so that Darcie could have her chance to shout at him for getting them all into this mess.

Midnight, SIS Headquarters, London: Wet and windy.

The Director of Regional Affairs in the Secret

Intelligence Service tapped his blotter as his head of station in Nairobi filled him in by video phone on the latest developments in the Michael Lock case. Outside his staff were in crisis mode: phones ringing, people coming and going at speed – but no one dare disturb the director.

'And what do you make of our girl, Agent Smith?' the director asked.

'Chip off the old block, sir.' The director smiled slightly. 'According to my deputy, she's spirited – she seems quite bright – but still, this might all be too much for her. Wouldn't it be better to get her out of the field?'

The director looked out of the window for a moment at the lights shimmering on the Thames. The events of the past few hours had drained him; he was desperate for a good result but aware his tools were limited. Risks had to be taken. Doing nothing for Michael Lock was not an option.

'Proceed with the plan. Break Darcie in gently: a small task after she's met the first target – something to get her thinking for herself. See what you make of her after you've met her properly.'

'All right, sir. We'll do what we can. But you do realise that it might be too late – too late for Michael, I mean?'

'Of course, I know that,' the director snapped. 'Now get some sleep and get on with your job. I believe you have a new recruit to train.'

After a restless night, Darcie was the first down to breakfast. For some reason the agents had only packed dresses and skirts so she was forced to put on the kind of clothes her mother insisted she wear to embassy events. Being men, they had probably assumed that was what girls of her age liked to wear but they were wrong in her case. Darcie had always felt happiest in jeans or light cotton shorts and T-shirts. Imagining what her mother would say was appropriate for breakfast at one of Nairobi's top hotels, she chose a strappy blue sundress, grimacing at herself in the mirror when she saw her reflection. It didn't seem right – but then nothing seemed right.

Feeling very exposed sitting on her own, Darcie took a table in the Thorn Tree Café near the acacia tree that served as a message board for travellers in Kenya. She passed the time reading the notes pinned haphazardly over it. *Bill, meet me in Mombasa. Jill from Oregon gone to Kampala.* She thought about leaving her own note: *Dad, where are you?* The old trunk twisted up through the café, roots hidden in the red earth of Africa just a few feet below the recent additions of concrete and tarmac. She ate her breakfast very slowly, not knowing what to do with the blank that was the rest of her day.

'Hey, it's Darcie, isn't it? I haven't seen you in the Stanley before.'

Darcie sat up from her half-doze over an orange juice. 'Oh, hi.'

It was Hugo Kraus – one of the seniors at her school and a big snob. He had never paid her any attention before. She was surprised he even knew her name. Only son of an old Kenyan (*Keen-yan,* Hugo always said) white family, he walked with the air of someone who did not know that colonial days were long gone. Now he was looking at her legs. 'What are you doing here?' he asked.

'What does it look like?' said Darcie wearily. 'I'm having breakfast.'

Hugo grinned. He was good-looking in a large-boned blond way and knew it. He assumed all girls would swoon at his feet. 'Try the *mandazis* – they're very good.' Dispensing this bit of wisdom with a wink, Hugo rejoined his father at a table with some other men. Mr Kraus looked over at her, said something to Hugo, then slapped him on the back, laughing.

Just to spite Hugo, Darcie almost refused the basket of little fried buns when the waiter offered them. But she changed her mind on catching their enticing smell. He was right – they were good. She ate four before getting up from the table. Hugo was still watching her as she walked past.

'Miss Lock?'

Darcie gave a start on hearing her name and span round to come face to face with a bellboy.

'Miss Lock? I've a message for you.'

Darcie took the pencil-written note.

Come to the High Commissioner's Residence. Ask for your mentor.

That's all it said. No name. Not even a time that she should arrive. They hadn't thought to send a driver for her. Didn't they realise she had no money and no transport?

Left with only one choice, she prepared herself for the long walk to Upper Hill Road. She changed into her trainers and wrapped a kikoy, a long length of brightly coloured cotton, around her shoulders. She didn't want to attract attention as a rich *mzungu* when she left the hotel foyer to step into the chaos outside.

Buses and *matatus* roared through the streets with careless abandon, horns blaring, sparkly decorations jiggling in windscreens in time to loud music. The uneven pavement was already hot and dusty. People stood in ragged lines at the bus stops, then moved swiftly to mob the doors as soon as they opened to squeeze on to the already packed vehicles. A young beggar held out a skeletal hand, eyes hopeless. Two plump women brushed past, their gossip punctuated with screams of laughter.

Darcie's sense of panic threatened to overwhelm her again as she plunged into the confusion of the crowds. What was she doing? This was insane. Shouldn't she just go to the airport and get out of here?

But what about Dad?

With Mom out of contact, she had no one to ask if she was doing the right thing by staying. Her parents had always claimed to have no close living relatives, though she no longer believed anything they had told her. For all she knew, she could have a whole raft of cousins in the Midwest, or grandparents sipping tea on a lawn in Hampshire. She realised just how isolated she was. Having taken it for granted that Winston and Tegla would always be around, she did not know how to contact them or even have a clear idea of where they lived. Her mates at school were all right for a game of football, but hardly the kind of people she could ask for advice about something like this. There was no one she could trust.

The crowds thinned as Darcie made her way up Haile Selassie Avenue. She was going against the tide of Kenyans walking into the city centre. Women strolled by with languid easy paces, one or two sparing a warm smile for the solitary girl heading the other way.

'*Jambo,*' said one, dressed like a bird of paradise in an orange and green kikoy. '*Habari?*'

'*Mzuri,*' replied Darcie, but she knew she had never felt less 'mzuri' in her life.

Tired as she was, the rhythm of slow walking became hypnotic and soothing. She had rarely walked far in Nairobi before and after ten minutes she'd paced her panic away. It was going to be all right. She'd find her dad. They'd rejoin Mom. *Hakuna matata.* She repeated it like a mantra – holding on to the words like a talisman to ward off paralysing fear.

Now she had calmed down, she was able to take in her surroundings. Like most expat kids, she'd gone everywhere in cars, hermetically sealed off from the Africa of the streets. She found she liked the sharp contrast of smells: sweet-scented bushes, steaming earth, petrol, rotting rubbish, and the endlessly varied sights of the roadside: shacks and shops, lush gardens and dusty markets. Despite the upset of the last twelve hours, she felt rooted in Kenya as she had never done in her old pot-plant life.

It wasn't until she reached a quiet stretch of road that she noticed the white Land Cruiser slowly approaching, a big cat stalking prey. Two men with dark glasses sat in the front; the one in the passenger seat had his arm dangling out the window, displaying a thick gold bracelet. Darcie's first thought was that he was stupid – a thief could easily make a grab for it. Then again, the man had the appearance of some-one you wouldn't like to upset: well muscled and tough. And he was still staring at her. She realised suddenly who was today's chosen victim. She had to get out of sight.

Turning off the road at the first opportunity, she

headed up a rutted driveway, planning to hide until the car had passed. The Land Cruiser followed her. Maybe this hadn't been such a bright idea after all. There was no one about. She might have done better on the highway. It was too late to go back now so she broke into a run, praying that this path would lead her to somewhere with people. The car sped up. She could hear the engine rumbling closer and closer. Sprinting round a corner, Darcie pelted into a yard full of vehicles. Tacked to the open door of a large shed, was a sign: *Jordan's Jolly Garage*. Two feet peeped out from underneath a BMW. She jumped over the outstretched legs and dived into the workshop, hiding behind a stack of tyres.

The crunch of wheels on the forecourt signalled the arrival of the Land Cruiser. Two doors slammed and footsteps approached her hiding place. Sweat trickled down her back. This was strange behaviour for muggers – if that's what they were.

'*Karibu*, my friends, what do you want?' It was a man's voice. There was a clatter of tools being dropped.

'If it is your car that needs fixing, I can see to it this afternoon, *hakuna matata*.'

The footsteps stopped. Darcie could see two long shadows stretching into the shed; they were joined by a third.

'I give you very good price. Nice car like that should be looked after by a good mechanic.'

'No, man. Our mistake,' said a deep voice. 'Took a wrong turn.'

'*Pole sana*. This road does not go anywhere. You will have to head back the way you came.'

Two of the shadows retreated, leaving only one in the doorway. Darcie heard an engine start.

'*Safari mzuri!*' called the man, giving a jaunty wave with a spanner. 'Do not forget: Jordan's Jolly Garage gives best price in Nairobi!'

His visitors called nothing out in return as the car growled angrily away like a lion deprived of its kill.

Darcie waited, wondering if she could slip past unseen when the mechanic returned to the BMW, but the shadow still hadn't moved.

'They have gone. You can come out now.'

He knew she was there. Darcie squeezed out from behind the tyres. A rough oily hand reached to assist her.

'*Asante,*' she said breathily.

A beanpole of a man stood looking down at her. Dressed in blue ripped overalls, a red scarf knotted at his neck, she guessed she was being inspected by Mr Jordan himself.

'You are running from bad men, my sister? That is *kali sana,*' he commiserated with her.

'Sorry about that,' she replied, lapsing into the English manners her father had drummed into her.

'Why were they following you?' Mr Jordan asked, his expression quizzical as he scratched his shaved head. Under the motor oil, he looked about thirty and had a wide, friendly smile.

Darcie shrugged. 'I don't know. I thought they might be muggers.'

'They are strange robbers to chase you up here.'

She had thought that too, but there seemed little point in saying so.

'They meant business, sister. One of them was armed.'

Darcie swallowed a gasp. She hadn't realised that they had a gun. Clearly, she couldn't risk going back to the road again. Perhaps she should get a taxi and ask the High Commission to pay on arrival.

'Can I borrow your phone? I want to call a cab.'

Mr Jordan wiped his hands on a rag. 'No need to do that. I run best taxi service in Nairobi.' He gestured to a wooden board nailed over the office door: *Jordan's Jolly Taxis*. Mr Jordan clearly had many strings to his bow. 'Where do you want to go?'

'The British High Commissioner's Residence.' She laced her hands together awkwardly. 'But I'm afraid I've no money on me.'

The mechanic inspected her again. A foreigner wandering around on her own and chased by a bunch of thugs. It didn't take a genius to work out she was in trouble.

'*Sawa, sawa,* damsels in distress are my speciality!' he said cheerfully. 'I will take you for free. Something tells me you are having a tough day.'

Darcie couldn't trust herself to reply without breaking down. She bit her lip and nodded.

'Follow me, sister. I am Jolly by the way.'

'Jolly?' Darcie asked as she jogged after him out to the forecourt.

'My mama's idea. Jolly Jordan.'

It was lucky Jolly had turned out to be a cheerful guy or the name would have been a burden. As it was, Darcie decided it suited him.

'I'm Darcie.'

'It is good to meet you, Darcie.'

The taxi was a battered Toyota that had seen better days. The door squeaked as he showed her into the back, but the engine sounded well enough when he turned the ignition.

'It is best that you hide, Darcie. Your *kali* friends are waiting for you,' Jolly said out of the corner of his mouth as they rounded the bend.

Darcie caught a glimpse of white before crouching down in the space between the front and rear seats. Jolly casually chucked a jacket into the back. She covered her head with it and curled up into a ball.

Who were these people? They were persistent if nothing else.

Jolly slowed as he approached the road. Darcie heard him wind down the window. Why was he stopping? He wasn't going to give her away, was he?

'Still lost, my friends? The city is that way.'

'Where are you going?' asked one of the men. Darcie guessed he was peering into the car right now.

Jolly tapped his roof. 'Jordan's Jolly taxi service, the best in Nairobi. I am off to the airport. Why? Do you need a ride?'

The man ignored the question. 'Did you see a *mzungu* back there?'

'No, brother. No white people. There is only my mean old Doberman.'

He wound up the window and pulled into the main road, chuckling. 'That should make them think twice before they turn the place over.' He put the radio on loud and began singing tunelessly.

Darcie waited a few moments. 'Is it safe to come out?'

'Yes, sister. They have not followed. They are probably creeping round my place right now, worried that a dog will jump out and bite their butts.'

'Do you have a Doberman?' Darcie passed him back his jacket.

'No, sister.' Jolly went off into a peal of laughter, swerving dangerously across the road.

By car, it took only a few minutes to reach the Residence. As she climbed out, Jolly pressed his card into her hand.

'Here, Darcie. I do not like bullies. If they bother you again, you remember old Jolly. I will come and get you.'

Darcie shook his hand. '*Asante sana,* Jolly. You're a real knight in shining armour.'

He gave her a grin. 'What better payment could a man ask than to have a pretty lady tell him that? You stay out of trouble, Darcie, *sawa*?'

With a final wave, Jolly drove off, leaving her standing outside the big iron gates. Darcie sighed, feeling much lonelier now he'd gone.

Stepping up to the intercom, she pushed the button. A grand white house glimmered at the end of a drive, the Union Jack fluttering on a flagpole in the forecourt. An air of Saturday calm lay about the place. Only the high commissioner's cherry red Jaguar sat waiting outside the main entrance. No voice challenged her as the gates swung open. She walked in and they closed behind her.

What now? She looked around, wondering where she should go. A gardener dressed in a white shirt and loose trousers passed by, pushing a barrow along a path by a border of exotic plants.

'Hey, excuse me!' called Darcie.

The gardener did not stop but beckoned over his head for her to follow. Darcie glanced up towards the main entrance to the residence, searching for someone else, anyone else, but there was no one in sight. Reluctantly, she followed him down a winding path between thick bushes on the compound perimeter. As the gardener manoeuvred the barrow to the right, Darcie saw with a jolt that he had a revolver strapped to his thigh, only half-hidden by the baggy cotton shirt.

'In there,' said the gardener, waving a hand towards a small white building set on its own in the compound grounds. Darcie now noticed that her guide had an earpiece in his ear. 'Good luck – you will need it.'

With that, the man picked up his barrow and continued his patrol.

Darcie mounted the short flight of steps and knocked on the wooden door. She was still feeling shaken by the adventure at Jordan's Jolly Garage. It had been stupid of them to put her on her own in the Stanley. Of course a lone western girl would attract trouble like bees to a honey pot. She'd be having words with them about that later.

Footsteps – the clicking of high heels – came from inside. She took a pace back as the door opened. There stood Gladys Smith, the elderly receptionist she had met once or twice. She had short white hair and blue-grey eyes. Her clothes were non-descript, smart but forgettable; only her jacket was distinguished by a brooch in the shape of a silver serpent. She was looking at a delicate gold watch on her wrist.

'Not bad. It only took you an hour to find us then,' she said, her voice brisk like the persistent tap of an old typewriter.

'Er, yes,' Darcie replied, looking over her shoulder to see if there was anyone else in the corridor behind her. In the shadows she thought she saw at least one man moving at the far end. 'Mrs Smith, could you tell my mentor that I've arrived?'

Gladys smiled up at her. She was very small – Darcie was already taller than her and she had by no means finished with growing. Gladys's eyes flickered with amusement. 'Of course. Come in.'

She stepped to one side, allowing Darcie into the hallway.

'You found us on your own then?' Gladys said conversationally as she led the way down the corridor. 'I'm glad to see you're not the sort who can't think for herself.'

Darcie wondered if she should say anything about

the men in the Land Cruiser but decided she'd save this until she met her mentor.

Gladys led Darcie into a beautiful room with French windows leading out on to a lawn. A swimming pool twinkled from behind the climbing tendrils of the passion flower that covered a trellis fence. The floor of the room was polished wood, the walls white, the ceiling high, adorned only by a slowly revolving brass fan. There was no furniture – just a large mirror on the wall opposite the French windows. In this space, Darcie would not have been surprised if ballet dancers in white tutus had burst into the room and begun to practise.

'Um, Mrs Smith, will you tell my mentor I'm here, please?' Darcie repeated when the lady showed no signs of moving.

'I have,' she replied shortly.

Darcie gaped.

'But –'

'I am your mentor, Darcie.'

This tiny, white-haired old woman with high-heeled

shoes was supposed to prepare her for the world of espionage? She must be kidding.

'Think I'm not up to the task?' Gladys rapped out, hooking Darcie with her steely gaze. 'Think that a girl like you won't learn anything from an old dear like me?'

She held out her wrinkled hand. Darcie looked at it for a second, simultaneously aware that someone had just entered the room behind her. She glanced over her shoulder: it was the British agent she'd met last night. The man nodded encouragingly to Darcie.

'Go on, dearie, you can give an old lady a hand, can't you?' said Gladys teasingly.

Darcie paused, then took the offered palm in her own. Before she knew what had happened, Gladys's feeble grip turned to iron. Darcie was twisted round and forced down into a headlock, staring now at the snake's-head beading on Gladys's shoes.

'First lesson – looks can be deceptive,' said Agent Smith.

Darcie could hear the British agent chuckling to himself.

'You can laugh,' said Gladys sharply as she released Darcie. 'I seem to remember I did the same to you on your first day in Nairobi – and you were already an agent of ten years' experience.'

The man strode forward and patted Darcie on the back.

'I see you've met your mentor, Darcie,' he said. 'Agent Smith. The boss. I'm her second-in-command – Agent Bulldog.'

Agent Smith. Agent Bulldog. And last night there had been Agent Eagle.

'These aren't your real names?' hazarded Darcie, rubbing her sore neck.

'Of course not,' snapped Gladys as if this was a silly question. 'No more than your father is Michael Lock and your mother Ginnie Lock.'

'Then who am I?' asked Darcie in bewilderment. 'I mean *really*?'

Gladys smiled. 'You're Darcie Lock, born at St Thomas's hospital, London, England on 19th March, fourteen years ago. I thought you knew that?'

'I did . . . I do . . . but nothing I knew seems to be true any more.'

'Well, that much is true – I promise you that. I was godmother at your christening so I can vouch for these facts.'

'My *godmother*?' Yet more news for Darcie.

'Of course. Michael and I were very close – he was one of my best. I hope his daughter proves to be as able as him.'

'I hope so too,' muttered Darcie, not liking the way Gladys used past tense to talk about her father.

'Good.' Businesslike again, Gladys clapped her hands together. 'Are you thirsty? You've passed the first test I set you – finding your own way here – so you deserve a reward.'

Darcie ran her tongue over her dry lips. 'Yeah, I'm thirsty.'

'Ben, can you bring Darcie and me some tea and mineral water? We'll be by the pool.'

Agent Bulldog nodded and withdrew.

'Follow me.'

Gladys led Darcie through the French windows.

'I've not seen this part of the residence before,' said Darcie. She could just make out the main building through the trees. The palatial home of the high commissioner was screened by a grove of banana plants and tree ferns. A vine with trumpet-shaped orange flowers and honey scent covered the buildings around the pool, clambering on to the roof of the changing rooms, almost burying them under greenery.

'No, you wouldn't've been allowed here. We're a separate operation. Colleagues with the diplomats but not under the high commissioner's control.'

'I see.'

Gladys plucked a passion fruit as they passed under the trellis arch and handed it to her. Darcie took the dark purple fruit tentatively, wondering if this was another test, fearing it might explode or poison her.

Gladys laughed a deep throaty chuckle. 'Good – I see you no longer take things at face value. But it's all right. There's nothing wrong with it – unless of course it's not quite ripe.'

Agent Smith sat down on a recliner by the pool and beckoned Darcie to sit beside her. She did so, but only to the point of perching on a corner. Using her nail, she burst open the passion fruit and sucked out the orange seeds. Gladys had chosen well: it was perfect – just right for eating.

'Now, Darcie, I'm going to talk straight with you.' Gladys took out a pair of sunglasses and settled back on the seat. 'Our operation is sunk unless you can find out what's happened to your father. We wouldn't normally dream of asking a teenager to help us but I can't risk blowing the cover of any more agents – we need someone no one suspects to ask a few questions. We don't want to do this but London agrees there's no other way. As your godmother, I should know better. Ginnie's going to kill me when she hears – and believe me, your mother's not a woman to cross.'

So her mom didn't know. This made Darcie feel slightly better as she hadn't liked to think her mother approved of dumping all this on her shoulders.

'But I guessed that you'd prefer to do something for

your father rather than be sent to safety. I was betting that you'd not want to think that, if only you'd stayed, you might have made a difference. Am I right?'

Darcie nodded.

'Good. Then it's my job to give you the best start I can. I've got the go-ahead to undertake your training myself.'

A tray rattled behind Darcie.

'You're lucky there, Darcie,' said Agent Bulldog. 'Gladys is the best in the business.'

Gladys waved away the compliment. 'But don't expect a soft ride just because you're a kid. In my eyes, from now on you're an agent. You'll abide by the rules and report to me. I'll praise you when you get it right, kick your behind when you get it wrong. Understood?'

Darcie shrugged as it slowly sank in. She wasn't sure she liked this fairy godmother of hers. Agent Bulldog handed her a glass of water and took a seat on the recliner.

'We're all really cut up about your dad,' he said. 'We know how hard it must be for you.'

'That's enough, Ben,' interrupted Gladys. 'The last thing Darcie needs now is a dose of sympathy. She's probably only just holding it together as things are. Any more of that and she'll possibly break down.'

As much as Darcie resented her stopping the first kind words she had heard since her world had been blown apart, Gladys was right. Agent Bulldog's sympathy had chipped away at the dam that was holding back her emotion.

'Sorry, ma'am,' he said. 'I'll shut up.'

'You do that. Now, have you got the file Michael put together for me?'

He nodded and produced a manila folder from under the tray.

'You'll spend this morning getting to grips with your brief,' continued Gladys. 'Take a swim if you like – you'll find some gear in the changing rooms. After lunch, I'll begin your physical training and give you your kit. Any questions?'

Darcie had hundreds of questions. She asked the first that floated to the surface. It was a stupid question really, but she needed something concrete in all this to hang on to.

'But what about school?'

Gladys sipped her water, wiping off the beads of condensation from the misted glass thoughtfully. 'Oh, you'll still be going to school. We need you to. Read the brief and you'll find out why.'

'And where will I stay?'

'Here, of course. We'll put the story about that your parents have been called away to a funeral in the States and that you're staying at the high commissioner's residence while they're gone. I've straightened it out with Sir Stephen. He and Lady Graham will keep the cover story going for you. Oh, and they expect you for tea at four by the way. It's got to look to the household staff as though you're really staying with them.'

'OK.'

'Right. You read that while I have a little doze in the sun. We'll talk about it when I wake up.'

Gladys tipped the chair back and appeared to settle almost at once into a sleep. Ben carried the tray back to the house and did not return. Darcie stared down at the file – the file that had caused both her parents to disappear. She took a deep breath, and flipped it open.

The first thing in the file was a picture of a tall, handsome Arab dressed in a white robe and headdress. He seemed vaguely familiar.

Abdul al Yaqoubi. Darcie recognised the handwriting on the back. Her father had noted the man's name in his distinctive neat script. Al Yaqoubi? Was this Kassim's dad? Darcie knew Kassim from the school football team. Now she came to think of it, the man in the picture shared his son's hawkish good looks, down to the intense brown eyes and strong features. She leafed through the notes: Omani family, shipping business based in East Africa, headquarters Nairobi with a fleet working out of Djbouti, Mombasa and Dar es Salaam. Possible use of legitimate activities to hide clandestine operations? No known links to extremists, but rumours connect him to terrorist cell responsible for bombing of the American Embassy in 1998.

Darcie found another photo – this one of Abdul al

Yaqoubi talking to an Asian woman in a restaurant. She was hunched forward over the table, hand curled round a glass, thick black hair falling forward over her face, hiding her features. Darcie turned to the back: *al Yaqoubi and contact* (*Regina Tsui? – ask Darcie to get details of home life*).

'That's because of the new niece – Pearl Cheng,' came Gladys's voice from behind the dark sunglasses.

'I thought you were asleep,' said Darcie.

'Appearances . . .'

'I know – can be deceptive,' Darcie finished for her. She remembered the new girl in her class, Pearl Cheng, an Asian girl, Hong Kong Chinese who had joined them only last week. Small, pretty, she had given Darcie one look and then ignored her, which Darcie had admired. That's how she would've liked to behave on her first day somewhere – to be so confident that she felt no need to rush into the business of making friends.

'Dad wanted me to find out about Pearl's aunt? He never mentioned it to me. Who is she?'

'Hong Kong fashion designer, recently established an operation here in Nairobi. Perfectly demure little thing, rarely seen out. Devoted aunt to rather a number of "nieces". Your classmate is the latest in a long line. These nieces live with her a few years and wind up married to some of the richest businessmen in the world. It is then not uncommon for said businessman to meet a sudden end, leaving his inconsolable wife in charge of his fortune. Oh, and did I mention, Madame Tsui is also deep in with the Triads and is a major drugs runner?'

'Nice.'

'One hundred per cent poison. We can't get near her. We've tried and failed. The last agent who attempted to penetrate Madame Tsui's empire ended up in bits – I don't think we ever found them all. That's when your father thought of asking you to befriend the new niece when she arrived – get in by the front door rather than the back for a change. We were talking it over when he disappeared. It's partly what gave me the idea of recruiting you.'

Darcie let this pass. She didn't feel 'recruited', whatever Gladys might think. She was just in this for her dad.

'So what's she doing meeting Abdul al Yaqoubi?'

'Good question. Your father thought he knew the answer.'

Darcie turned back to the file and came across another photo, this one of a group of white men sitting round a table under a tree.

'I know these people. I saw them this morning. One's Hugo Kraus's father.'

'I'm glad to see your stay at the Stanley at HMG's expense was not entirely wasted,' Gladys commented drily. 'Did Hugo like the dress?'

'How did you know about that?'

Gladys shook her head slightly. 'Men – boys – like Hugo are so predictable. I knew that when I told them to pack only pretty clothes. I was hoping your paths would cross this morning – it's a regular venue for Kenya's finest farmers to meet and moan about the state of the country.'

'But what have they to do with this?'

'Your father was sure that the traffickers have a base near Nairobi, but not in Nairobi itself – somewhere where they can hide large amounts of gear, not to mention people, that they don't want the authorities to notice. He had reason to suspect Mr Kraus and his cronies.'

'What reason?'

'For one, they're all cranks – right-wingers of the most extreme sort,' Gladys said. 'They're the kind of people who'd have enough armaments to equip a private army and dream of returning Kenya to the good old days when their sort ruled the roost. Your dad told me he was following up a lead but it was too early for specifics. He thought they were aiming to destabilise the current president of Kenya – but with their sort that could all be wishful thinking. Most of these groups turn out to be harmless – usually end up turning their guns on themselves.'

Darcie read her way through the rest of the material. Much of it she didn't understand – clumps of financial transactions and shipping notices. It appeared to tell a story but not one that she could follow.

'A real dog's breakfast, isn't it?' commented Gladys. 'But you'll be pleased to know that your father managed to reduce it to some simple facts. Someone is using East African ports to smuggle illicit goods – that's people, drugs and guns – in and out of the region. The networks involved are global but the weak spot is local. The big boss is here. The operation must be protected by someone in government to have got this far. Michael thought that these three could lead him to the main man. It looks as if he was right, but unfortunately for us, your father couldn't get away to tell us what he had found at the end of the trail. And we must know what he discovered: we want the Ringmaster, the person calling the shots – not the clowns. We're on the back foot now; I need you to shift the balance in our favour.'

'What do you want me to do?' Darcie had a brief absurd image of herself abseiling down the side of a building, bursting into a room full of megalomaniacs intent on destroying the world.

'Get to know these people – find out as much as you can about them – find out which one your father met yesterday.'

Gladys made it sound easy. Darcie shifted her recliner into the shade as the sun dazzling off the pool was giving her a headache – or maybe that was down to what Gladys was telling her.

'And how do I do that?'

'Use your contacts at school. Remember, Darcie: to the world you look like a kid missing her parents. Invitations should be showering in to keep you occupied. Make use of them. Make sure you're invited by the right people.'

Darcie stared out across the lawn wilting in the noon heat and remembered Pearl's aloof gaze on her first day.

'But I hardly know any of them.'

'Well, that's all going to change. One of the last things your father did was to invite them and their families to the QBP for us to take a closer look at how they behaved together.'

'QBP?'

'A quaint British tradition.' Gladys gave a sour smile. 'Our national day – the Queen's Birthday Party. It's on Monday. As house guest of the high commissioner, you'll be there too – on duty. And you'll have help. I've primed your mother's friend, Doreen Clutterbuck, to take you under her wing.'

Darcie stared at Gladys. 'Does she work for the CIA as well?'

Agent Smith gave a snort of laughter. 'Heavens, no. Not all your allies will be agents, Darcie. She just has the kind of character that'll assume waifs and strays like you to be her responsibility. She'll have the entire expat community lining up to offer you hot meals. You just need to steer her in the right direction. She'll make short work of Yaqoubi and Kraus, if I know her. Madame Tsui is more of a challenge, but Doreen'll give it a go if you nudge her.

'Now, you finish reading that. Have a swim. Sleep if you want – you look done in. I'll come and fetch you in a few hours for your training session.'

Gladys got up and disappeared back into the villa. The swimming pool did look very inviting. Darcie put the papers to one side and explored the changing room. Her red swimming costume lay on top of a towel, yet more evidence of her life being ransacked by others. She changed into it and dived into the pool, hoping that the cold water would punch the unpleasant memories of the last twelve hours out of her. A strong swimmer, she kept up a steady tally of lengths, thinking through everything she had learned from the file. Pearl. Kassim. Hugo. Doors leading to her father perhaps? She didn't know two of them well, the third she didn't like. This wasn't going to be easy.

Towelling herself off, she sank on to the recliner. Sleep stole over her as she relaxed in the shade of the passion flower arbour. It seemed no time at all until Agent Bulldog returned with a tray of sandwiches.

'Thanks,' she said, curling her legs under the towel out of sight.

'Call me Ben.'

'OK, Ben.'

'Her Nibs is waiting,' Ben said, nodding back to the house. 'I wouldn't eat too much if I were you. She'll probably have you suspended from the ceiling in two ticks.'

Darcie ate a couple of sandwiches with Ben. Then she wrapped the towel around her waist and headed back to the villa.

Gladys was standing in front of the mirror in the practice room, dressed in a loose white jacket and trousers, fastened by a black belt. A sports bag lay at her feet.

'Right, first your kit.' She kicked the bag over to Darcie. 'Take a look. Tell me what you see.'

Darcie knelt over the bag and reached to unzip it.

'Hold on. Tell me what you see.'

She sat back on her heels, hand hovering over the zip. 'I see a black Puma sports bag.'

'Anything else?'

She remembered her lesson – appearances can be deceptive – and took a closer look.

'The tag is bigger than normal. It's got a small

red light, like you get on a car key.'

'Good. Put your thumb on the flat part and press.'

Darcie did as instructed. The light changed from red to green.

'It's now got your thumbprint recorded. You can open it.'

'And what if I'd tried to before?'

'You wouldn't have been able to. The zip is now locked and will only work for you. The material is kevlar – the same stuff they use for bullet-proof jackets – very hard to cut through.'

Darcie hesitated before digging inside. Gladys arched one eyebrow.

'Go on.'

Her fingers curled around a small object. She pulled it out. It looked like one of the latest generation mobile phones.

'What's this?'

'Your phone, of course.'

'Oh.' She was disappointed. She'd been expecting something more exciting.

'The address book has all our numbers for you to report in. I'm under Aunt Flo. Agent Bulldog is your dentist. If you need to reach us in an emergency, just press 999 – it'll send us a distress signal. We can track the phone wherever it is, so try not to get separated from it.'

Darcie slipped the phone back into the bag and continued to rifle through the contents. She pulled out a dark bundle.

'A new twist on the little black dress for my female operatives,' Gladys explained drily. 'Every girl should have one. The neck pulls up at the back to cover your face. The material stretches so it's good if you have to run or climb. The perfect snooping gear – normal enough not to arouse suspicion, converts in a second. There's a matching hairband which we've fitted with a microphone so we can listen in.'

Darcie said nothing but continued to pull out a camouflage jacket, a Swiss army knife, army rations and a canteen. The last thing was an aerosol of insect spray. She took the lid off to try it out.

'I wouldn't do that if I were you,' Gladys cautioned. 'It's pepper spray. Another deterrent. Spray this in the face of an attacker and he won't thank you – but neither will he be able to see you make your getaway.'

Darcie sat back looking at her haul.

'Is this it?'

'Why? What were you expecting – an Aston Martin?'

'That'd be nice.' Darcie returned her smile. 'I don't know what I was expecting.'

'Darcie, you need to forget everything you've seen in films about spies. We're not licensed to kill. I don't have a budget that stretches to gizmos and gadgets to get you out of implausible situations. That all belongs to fantasy. Toys for the boys. We've kitted you out so that you can defend yourself if someone attacks – knowing Nairobi it's more likely to be a mugger than anyone in that file. You've got gear to help you sniff around a little but we don't want you to take any chances. Your own wits are better at keeping you out of trouble than anything we give you.'

'I already ran into trouble on my way here,' Darcie

admitted. 'They might've been muggers, but they acted very oddly.'

'What?' Gladys swung round sharply to face her.

'I was followed by two men in a white Land Cruiser. They were very persistent.'

'That shouldn't have happened,' Gladys muttered with a frown. 'I'll get Ben on to it – see if we can find out who they were.'

'Do you think they have anything to do with my dad?'

'Very possibly. If so, it's the first lead we've had. Let us know immediately if you see them again.' Gladys was silent for a moment, occupied by her thoughts. 'I'm sorry that happened – I miscalculated. I should've sent Ben to fetch you.'

Darcie shrugged. Memories of this morning's adventure were no longer so frightening. If anything, what she remembered most was Jolly Jordan and his braying laugh. 'It doesn't matter – I got away and it's given you something to go on. But, as it seems someone's interested in me, perhaps you'd better tell me how to protect myself.'

'I'm glad you asked.' Gladys snapped back into action. 'There's only one rule: be cleverer than your opponent. Don't get caught. If you get caught, don't let them get suspicious. If they're suspicious, make sure they underestimate you and use that to your advantage.'

'How?'

'Get them off balance.'

With a lightning kick, she struck Darcie on the shoulder and sent her flying.

'See – you weren't ready – you'd dropped your guard,' she said. 'That was stupid. Now, get back how you were and I'll try it again. This time you know it's coming.'

With a groan, Darcie crouched back by the bag, watching Gladys's feet. She only saw her elbow slicing down towards her a split second before it struck. She twisted so that it glanced off her back.

'Good!' said Gladys, straightening up. 'A bit late, but your reaction was fast. And you're still on your feet. You could have made life very difficult for me by now if you'd struck back. The key is not to give your attacker the chance. In life, most people will be bigger and stronger than you. I'll show you a few self-defence techniques – good for any woman anywhere to know – but that's all we'll have time to do. Get yourself changed and I'll call Ben.'

During the next hour, Gladys showed Darcie how to break a hold if grabbed from behind, how to fall, where to kick. Darcie felt black and blue with bruises but Ben had barely broken into a sweat as he deflected Darcie's counter-attacks. For all Gladys's instructions, Darcie had not managed to throw him once.

'Pathetic,' barked Gladys from the sidelines. 'He's a man – not a mountain. Even a girl your size should be able to floor him! You just need to do what I say!'

Panting hard, Darcie turned to face her instructor, anger fizzing inside. 'It's all right for you to say. But to me, he might as well be a mountain. Aargh!'

The cry came as she sailed over backwards. Ben had taken advantage of the distraction to throw her again.

'I've had enough,' Darcie said, scrambling to her

feet. 'I don't want to play your games any more.' She could sense that Ben was creeping up on her. 'I'm completely rubbish at this. I want out.'

Ben hesitated behind her. Darcie spun round, ducked under his left arm to hook his leg from under him. Agent Bulldog crashed to the floor, face in the dust.

'Excellent!' called Gladys. 'You're finally learning. You got him off balance with your "I'm giving up" routine and pressed home your advantage. That's exactly what I'm trying to teach you. You won't beat a man like Ben in a straight fight – you have to do something to even out the odds.'

Darcie accepted the praise, though she knew it was not deserved. She didn't want to admit that her threat to throw in the towel had not been a routine: she'd meant it. Perhaps that didn't matter now. It had worked hadn't it?

5

The high commissioner and his wife did not know what to make of the lanky teenager they had been asked to host. Their elegant home, with its five large reception rooms furnished by the Foreign Office with English antiques, exotic flower arrangements and priceless oil paintings, had seen many odd characters over the years, but perhaps none so strange as this quiet girl. Darcie was sitting on the other side of the table on the veranda, cup of Earl Grey in hand, sipping it slowly, yet they could tell something was very wrong. For a start, their guest was dressed in a short flowered dress which showed her arms and legs were covered in new bruises. As the butler replenished their cups, Sir Stephen shifted unhappily in his wicker chair. He had a daughter the same age as Darcie at school in Cheltenham. He didn't like this business one bit. Gladys Smith had no right to exploit the child. If it had been in his power, he would have put the girl on a plane and called for more conventional assistance to find the missing man. Perhaps that was what he still should do, even though his blunt telegrams had received equally curt refusals from London. He knew the stakes must be very high if the Friends were willing to risk the child, but still . . .

'So, Darcie, how are you getting on with them over there?' he asked kindly, once the butler had departed.

'Fine, thanks.' She wasn't looking at him but at the rim of her bone china tea cup.

'I can't help noticing that you seem . . . how can I put it? . . . a bit battered.'

Darcie shrugged. 'It looks worse than it feels. They're giving me some self-defence classes. It's a good idea. You know how Nairobi is . . . '

'I see.' Sir Stephen glanced over at his wife, cueing her to say something.

'Darcie, my dear, we're worried about you. We think you'd be better off taking a flight home to Britain,' said Lady Graham in a soft voice. 'Biscuit?'

Darcie shook her head – a double refusal. 'I don't have a home to go to.'

'You could go to your mother,' Lady Graham persisted.

'And leave Dad on his own?' The girl said it as if the suggestion was mad.

Sir Stephen coughed. 'I don't like to speak ill of my colleagues, but I think you should be warned that they have a habit of never being quite straight with us. It goes with the territory you might say. I don't know what they've told you, but I would bet my life that they're keeping you deliberately in the dark. For a start, never believe them if they tell you what they're asking you to do isn't dangerous. Of course it is. I'd never forgive myself if something happened to you.'

'And I'd never forgive myself if I didn't try to do something to help Dad.' The girl's voice was calm – a little cold even. Perhaps she was still in shock? Hardly surprising considering all she had been through in the last twenty-four hours.

'Well, if you change your mind, let me know and I'll

personally ensure you're on the first flight out of here,' the high commissioner said. He just hoped she'd come round to his way of thinking before this got out of hand. 'Make yourself at home while you're with us. We've given you our daughter's bedroom – we thought you'd like that. We've a busy week ahead what with the QBP and the royal visit. The prince and his party will be arriving at the weekend, but that shouldn't affect you. It's not an official trip, just a brief holiday.'

'Thank you. I'll try and keep out of the way.'

'Is there anything you need, Darcie?' Lady Graham asked.

'Well, I don't suppose you could find out what's happened to my normal clothes – my jeans and sports stuff? I've only got dumb dresses and skirts.'

Lady Graham smiled. 'It's the least I can do, though you do look very nice in that one.'

'Mom's idea of smart.' Darcie looked away, aware her eyes had filled with tears on the mention of her mother.

'But you can't always be smart, can you? Comfortable matters more.'

'That's right.' Back under control, she turned to her hosts and smiled. She liked them both very much: they were on her side. 'Thanks for allowing me to stay.'

'We wouldn't have it any other way,' said Sir Stephen. 'We wanted to bring you here last night but Mrs Smith insisted you stayed at the Stanley.' He blew on his tea, waving the steam away. 'Be careful, Darcie, she's playing a dangerous game and you've become one of her pawns.'

'I'll remember.' Darcie put her cup down. 'Can I make a confession?'

The high commissioner sat up. Had she changed her mind already?

'I don't really like Earl Grey. Can I have fruit juice?'

Darcie returned to the villa that evening for more lessons, leaving Sir Stephen and Lady Graham discussing final arrangements for the QBP. This time Ben was schooling her in surveillance techniques.

'What you've got to understand, Darcie,' he said as he set up the computer screen, 'is that the life of an intelligence operative is nothing like what you've seen on TV. Much of it is tedious leg-work for little or no result. We do three main things: Befriending – that's getting to know key contacts and obtaining information from them, Infiltrating – entering organisations that are of interest to us, and Surveillance – bugging, use of satellite imagery, or just plain old tailing. Nothing beats the human touch despite all these fancy listening devices they dream up. B.I.S. – that's our business, you might say.' He chuckled. Darcie smiled politely.

'As you probably know, all intelligence-gathering methods are flawed. The fallout over Iraq proved that much to the world. Not a glorious episode. We're all hungry for an intelligence success to put that failure out of everyone's mind, I can tell you. Michael and Ginnie's work here was the nearest we've come so far. We're gutted that it's fouled up.'

Not as gutted as I am to lose my parents, she thought sourly.

'You see, Darcie, spies have to learn that you can have friends in high places but they may not tell you the truth. You might start to see things in sat images that you want to be there but aren't. You've got to learn to keep an open mind and don't trust anyone. I could go on, but I expect you'd prefer it if I got down to the business of your mission.'

Darcie grimaced at the word *mission* and chewed the top of her pencil.

'Befriending – well, you know your three targets: Pearl, Kassim and Hugo. Couldn't be easier: they're all around your age and at your school: you've been handed them on a plate.'

Oh yeah? What he hadn't mentioned was that they'd probably decided long ago she was way below their league and want nothing to do with her. Had he forgotten what it was like to be a teenager?

'Infiltrating. That's the next step. All we want you to do is get your foot in their door, have a sniff around and tell us if you find anything that smells of your dad. The slightest thing is of interest to us. More than usual curiosity as to what he did at the High Commission, for example. We're guessing that the ones who snatched him will be pretty anxious to find out how much we know. They'll be as interested in you as you are in them.

'Agent Smith has left something to help you gain access to the right people,' Ben continued. He put a make-up bag on the table in front of her. Darcie hesitated, making Ben smile. 'Go on, open it.'

She unzipped it and poured out on to the table a selection of top brand cosmetics – mascara, eye-shadow, foundation, lipstick.

'What do they do?' she asked, unscrewing a pot and giving it a sniff. 'Truth drugs or something?'

'Get real, Darcie,' laughed Ben. 'They're just the usual war-paint. As for what you do with them, that's your department. The boss thinks you need to glam up a bit for Pearl and Hugo. You'll find we've even run to a few new items in your wardrobe – almost emptied our money bags for the year and it's only June. I don't know how she swung it with London.' He shook his head, tutting.

'New items?'

'Designer stuff. The Kraus crowd buy the best, so you must too. And Madame Tsui's a fashion designer as you know – one of the dresses is her label. Her Nibs wants you to wear it for the QBP – as an ice-breaker with our Asian friends.'

Darcie felt goose pimples on her arms. 'I can't do this, Ben. They all know me – I'm the class tomboy – not one of them.'

'Course you can do it, Darcie. It's your disguise. What did you think we'd provide you with: a curly wig and Inspector Clousseau mac? You've got to make them see you as you want them to see you. They'll probably be looking at you properly for the first time in any case. We want them to see a sophisticated chick who they would like to hang out with. The sport thing you do is cute but . . .' He left the sentence hanging.

Darcie was feeling angry. She didn't do a 'sport thing' – this was her. If Gladys and Ben had their way, they'd turn her into the kind of girl she despised – the kind of girl who hung on Hugo's arm at break and got invited to all the right social events.

They had a point.

'OK. You make me look like some dippy chick. What next?'

Ben grinned. 'Surveillance. Let me show you how it's done.'

6

06.30, Nairobi: Hot and humid with thundery outbreaks of rain.

Darcie woke on Monday morning with a feeling of doom. This afternoon was the QBP. If she was going to 'glam up' she'd better prepare the way at school today.

Opening the make-up bag, she set about her face with a skill her mom would have approved of. Ginnie Lock may have neglected to tell her many essential things, but she had made sure her daughter knew how to be well groomed. Darcie was surprised to feel how fiercely she was missing her mom right now. They rubbed each other up the wrong way when together, but just at the moment Darcie wanted nothing more than one of her mom's hugs. Having held her tears back so long and tried to be brave all weekend, she gave in. At first the crying felt a relief, but then she got angry with herself. This wasn't going to save Dad. She crumpled up her last tissue and looked up into the mirror. She was a wreck with mascara running down her cheeks. With renewed determination, she wiped the smudges away and repaired the damage.

Finally, Darcie brushed her hair, deciding to leave it loose. Time to face her public.

Joel, Sir Stephen's Kenyan driver, dropped her at the school gate. 'I'll pick you up at three, miss,' he said as he opened the door for her to get out. The red Jag purred away, attracting many curious and appreciative stares from the students.

Darcie was about to walk in when she heard a whistle behind her. She knew who it was even before she turned round.

'Winston!'

Her friend was lounging against a tree opposite her school, bouncing a ball lazily. She swiftly crossed the road.

'What are you doing here?' she asked.

'*Jambo*, Darcie!' Winston's smile was relaxed and unruffled. He started to bounce the ball from knee to knee. 'They would not let me see you so I thought I would come and find you.'

'You'll get in trouble.' Winston's school was a half hour's walk away – he was missing his lessons to see her.

Winston shrugged. 'What is happening, Darcie? Why are you not allowed to stay at home?'

Darcie flushed. What could she tell him? She wanted to tell him the truth.

'Something's gone wrong. Mom and Dad have had to go away.'

He stopped bouncing the ball and looked at her strangely. 'Is it true what they are saying?'

'I don't know. What are they saying?'

'That your dad was caught doing something bad – selling visas.'

'What!' Darcie then remembered her father's cover story for the smuggling ring. How had Winston heard this? 'Who told you that?'

'The men who made us pack up and leave. They said we would not be seeing any of you again. They told us to keep our mouths shut. Mama was furious with them.'

'Oh.' Giving herself a moment to think, Darcie took the ball from him and spun it on her finger. If it fell, she'd tell him the truth. It didn't: it twirled on a perfectly balanced axis. She tossed it into the air and caught it. 'Look, I don't know what's going on. No one's telling me anything. All I know is that there's trouble.'

'There is trouble all right.' Winston nodded over to a red-faced man approaching them with the ferocity of a charging bull.

'Darcie Lock! What do you think you're doing? You're supposed to be at registration.' Mr Franklin, the headmaster, cast a suspicious look at Winston. His school was very international but he could tell at a glance that the Kenyan boy was from a different social bracket to his privileged pupils. It would not do to have one of his girls seen fraternising with that sort. 'Haven't you got somewhere to go, young man?'

Darcie resented the teacher's rudeness to her friend but knew she'd only get Winston into trouble if she lingered. She threw her friend the football. 'Bye, Winston. See you.'

'I will come again soon, *sasa*?' Winston called after her as the teacher shepherded her into the school. 'Mama wants to see you too.'

Darcie waved an acknowledgement. She still didn't know quite how to take the fact that Winston and Tegla suspected her father of the worse kind of corruption. Why had the spies had to do that to her father's reputation?

Darcie was too preoccupied to notice the interest her new appearance had aroused in the girls in her class as they queued outside their classroom. The first lesson was maths taken by Mrs Pringle – a teacher known for her short temper. She was bustling now in front of the whiteboard, writing up some equations. The blinds were down on the window, the ceiling fan hummed. Darcie had chosen a seat so she could feel the breeze on her arms and back of her neck. She was just beginning to relax when she recognised what the teacher was writing – it was the homework she'd been set on Friday and completely forgotten about. What could she say? That her parents had gone missing and that she'd been too busy training as a secret agent to bother with schoolwork? That wouldn't wash with Mrs Pringle.

'Right now, class. Let's crack on with these.' Mrs Pringle paused to fan herself with the textbook. 'Tell me your solutions. Pearl, what's the answer to number one?'

Pearl Cheng rose in her seat. Remembering what she'd read in the file, Darcie watched her closely. Did Pearl know what Madame Tsui really was? Had she any idea about the future her 'aunt' had planned for her?

'x equals 6y,' said Pearl in a soft, husky voice.

Mrs Pringle smiled. 'Very good. I can see you've made an excellent start with us.' The teacher's eye travelled around the class and fell on Kassim al Yaqoubi, yawning at the back. 'Kassim, do you have an answer to number two?'

'I had a stab at it, miss,' said Kassim with a

captivating smile, 'but I'm not sure I got it right. Is it 9?'

Darcie joined in with the friendly laughter that rippled round the room. Kassim had the talent of making you forgive him even before he made a mistake. He never did his homework when there was a football to kick around but somehow the teachers let him get away with murder, perhaps because he always seemed so charmingly apologetic about his failings. Darcie's smile faded: what else might he be getting away with? Did he know anything about her father?

Mrs Pringle shook her head. 'A bit of a stab in the dark, Kassim, I'm afraid. Let's ask someone else. Darcie?'

Darcie sat up with a jolt. She stood up, brushing her hair out of her face. 'I'm very sorry, Mrs Pringle, but I didn't have time to do my homework.'

Mrs Pringle frowned. 'That's not like you, Darcie.' The teacher's eyes travelled over the new look of one of her most studious pupils, resting disapprovingly on the make-up and flopping hair. She recognised the signs: first you have a well-behaved girl, then the hormones kick in and they get obsessed with boys and fashion, losing all interest in schoolwork. She would have to nip this in the bud. 'You're approaching your GCSEs: you can't afford to slack off now. I'm afraid you'll have to stay behind and do the homework in detention.'

Darcie gulped. She couldn't do that! She'd miss the QBP. Here she was: a secret agent and in danger of missing the first stage of her mission because she had been put in detention! James Bond didn't have to put up with this.

'But, miss, one of my relatives died last Friday. My parents had to go away suddenly. I think the high commissioner or one of his people telephoned the school about it.'

Mrs Pringle's expression softened. 'Oh, I'm sorry to hear that. Why didn't you say so at first? Sit down, Darcie. We'll talk about the homework after the lesson.'

Darcie sighed with relief as she slumped in her chair. The lie had tripped off her tongue easily.

At least, *I hope it is a lie* she thought with a sick dread, as she wondered once again what had happened to her father.

When Darcie arrived back from school, she found the high commissioner's garden decked out in its party outfit of red, white and blue bunting, pots of lush plants and flowers, and a marquee with tables laden with strawberries and cream. She made her way to her room to change, seeing through the French windows that the lawn had been invaded by the Highland Band of the Scottish Division, currently on tour in East Africa. The high commissioner had forewarned her over breakfast that he had managed to engage their services for the afternoon. The soldiers paraded like exotic animals over the green turf in their uniform of kilts and red tufted bearskins, practising the 'Skye Boat Song' on their bagpipes and drums. A number of local staff had stopped work to watch as the men slow-marched up and down in strict order; the Kenyans were as interested in them as any tourist in the red-robed Masai warriors to be seen at the Bomas a few miles away.

Shutting the door on the wailing of the pipes, Darcie changed into the outfit designed by Madame Tsui, that had been selected for her. It was a backless silk dress, gold at the neck, deepening to red at the hem. Looking in the mirror, Darcie felt it was like being dressed in a flame, beautiful but somehow dangerous. She twisted her hair up on top of her head and fastened it with a matching silk flower, not quite believing what she saw. She looked so sophisticated, not herself at all, except for the fading bruises on her arms and shins. Covering these with foundation, the last evidence of her tomboy self was blotted out. She didn't like it.

Darcie slipped in at the back of the living room where Sir Stephen was giving his diplomatic staff their last-minute briefing. Perched on the Chippendale furniture, they had the air of troops just about to go into battle on this the biggest day in the year for the British High Commission.

'We're not expecting the president, but if he turns up, make sure he is conducted straight through to where I will be waiting in the marquee. Same for the vice-president, who we believe *will* put in an appearance. John, don't forget to press the minister for trade for news about the railway contract. Felicity, keep the old president away from the government ministers. We don't want a repeat of what happened at the Dutch national day.'

A titter of laughter went around the room.

'Right. Any questions? No? Good. Action stations.'

The meeting broke up and Gladys came over to Darcie.

'You look perfect. Everything all right?' she asked, taking the girl's arm and leading her out to the garden. A few members of the British business community had already arrived and were enjoying the free champagne. A string quartet played on the terrace. The highlanders had disappeared for the moment.

'I think so.' Darcie smoothed her dress nervously.

'You won't need to do much. Just be nice to your targets. Mrs Clutterbuck will do the rest. I've asked her to come early. Can you see her?'

Darcie was about to shake her head when a shriek rose up behind them.

'There you are, Darcie!'

Darcie turned only to be buried in a rhinestone-studded jacket, her skin clutched in silver talons.

'So sorry to hear about your grandma. Is your mom OK? But look at you! You look fantastic!' exclaimed Doreen as she took in her charge's changed appearance. 'Growing up at last, hey? Got your eye on a boy?'

Darcie blushed and mumbled a denial.

'Sweet as candy, isn't she? I could just eat her myself!' the Texan declared turning to Agent Smith. 'I suppose she gets the shyness from her father. So, how have you done since our last little chat, Gladys?'

'I've managed to arrange for Darcie to stay here, Doreen, but, as you know, Sir Stephen and Lady Graham are very busy people.' Darcie could have sworn that Gladys took on a hunch and a feeble quaver to her voice as she spoke to the American. 'It'll be very lonely for her. If you could approach the parents of some of her particular friends for me, I'd be most grateful.'

'Don't you worry, honey, I'll see that Darcie is well looked after. You Brits are sure doing your share; it's about time we Yanks pulled a few strings for her.' Doreen threaded her arm through Darcie's. 'And I dare say, with you looking a million dollars, honeybun, we'll have people queuing up round the block to have you over.'

Doreen steered Darcie over to the strawberries. 'Look, there's your sweetheart now. Let's start with him.'

'Sweetheart?'

'You don't have to pretend with Doreen. There are no secrets between your mom and me.'

That's what she thought.

'Little old Gladys let slip that you'd fallen for a certain someone,' Doreen said coyly.

Please God, let it not be Hugo, thought Darcie. She couldn't bear thinking of Doreen dropping unsubtle hints about him in his presence. He hardly needed encouragement to think every girl found him irresistible.

'I admit it's a challenge even for me, but I said I'd try. I can't say I agree with how they treat their women, but maybe this young man is different,' continued Doreen. Her hand hovered over a champagne glass before plumping for an orange juice. 'Don't want to make the wrong impression by flaunting alcohol in front of them, do we? Look, there they are. My, I can see why you fell for him.' She pushed her sunglasses on to the back of her head. 'Omar Sharif, eat your heart out.'

Darcie raised her eyes in time to see Doreen making a beeline for Kassim. He was standing with his father and mother all in a depressed huddle, probably wondering what on earth they had done to get invited to the British national day. She hurried to catch up with Doreen.

'Mr and Mrs Yaqoubi, how delightful to meet you at long last,' breezed Doreen. 'I've heard so much about your son from Darcie here.'

Darcie blushed and looked at her feet. She could feel three pairs of dark eyes staring at her.

'Have you indeed, Mrs . . . ?' replied Mr Yaqoubi.

'Clutterbuck, Doreen Clutterbuck. My husband's here with the American Embassy. Mrs Yaqoubi, we don't see you at the International Women's Group, do we? We can always do with a few more recruits.'

Mrs Yaqoubi began to whisper something shyly in reply.

'It's all women, you know – except for the Norwegian Ambassador's husband but we've got him very well-trained. Adorable man. We do simply truckloads of good work.' Doreen continued to expand on the theme of the planned bring-and-buy-sale in aid of a local orphanage, not requiring anyone else to take part in the conversation. Darcie looked up at Kassim. He had been watching her but immediately turned away, taking a sudden interest in a flower arrangement over his mother's head. Darcie wondered if he was embarrassed to have heard that she had supposedly talked about him at home.

Doreen was working her way round to her point. 'I do so think we international women must stick together, don't you agree, Mrs Yaqoubi? Watch out for each other's children in a crisis and that kind of thing?' Mrs Yaqoubi nodded vaguely, looking deeply uncomfortable. 'Did you know, my good friend, Darcie's mom, has just lost her mother?'

'I'm very sorry to hear that,' said Mrs Yaqoubi in a barely audible voice, looking nervously at her husband.

'That's exactly what I said. So all us moms are taking it in turn to have Darcie over to our place to offer her a bit of home cooking. Now, I've been told that hospitality is a great tradition of your people. As she's friendly with your boy, I thought you'd like to take your turn. Tomorrow maybe? I haven't found anyone to look after her on that night yet and we can't leave poor little old Darcie on her own now, can we?'

Mr Yaqoubi had a dark look on his face as he watched his wife being expertly railroaded into offering a strange girl a place at their dinner table.

'Mrs Clutterbuck,' he began imperially.

'Doreen,' she smiled back at him undaunted.

'I don't think you quite understand . . .'

Darcie felt her blush deepen to crimson. Dressed like a flame already, she was surprised she didn't burn up like a Roman candle.

'Oh, did I mention that Darcie is very good with children? I hear you have two mighty fine girls. Twins, am I right?' interrupted Doreen.

'Yes, but . . . '

'Well, Darcie could entertain them for you. I'm sure they'd love to meet her.'

Doreen opened her big blue eyes wide, fixing Mr Yaqoubi in her gaze. Darcie wished the ground would open up and swallow her. She hadn't realised that working for the Secret Service would be so embarrassing.

'Mrs Clutterbuck,' Mr Yaqoubi began again, the refusal obvious in his tone of voice. 'It would not be appropriate.'

Kassim moved to touch his father on the arm. He cast an odd look at Darcie: was it sympathy? 'It's OK, Abu.'

Mr Yaqoubi was surprised. 'You know this girl?' he asked sharply.

'She's in my class. Plays in the girls' football team,' Kassim said. 'She's not bad – for a girl.'

Kassim smiled at her. Was he teasing?

'Thanks, Kassim,' Darcie said, returning the smile hesitantly. 'You're not bad either – for a boy.'

'So tomorrow it is then,' said Doreen brightly, grabbing Darcie's elbow and pulling her away before Mr Yaqoubi had a chance to refuse. 'That's very kind of you. And I'll see you at the International Women's Group then, Mrs Yaqoubi?'

They made a rapid getaway. Darcie risked a glance over her shoulder and saw Kassim talking to his father, hand on his sleeve – he seemed to be trying to placate him. She was grateful, if a little puzzled, that Kassim had spoken up for her when Doreen's clumsy approach had been going off the rails. He had no hesitation about inviting her home – unlike his father. If Mr Yaqoubi had abducted her dad, Kassim appeared to know nothing about it and had no reason to be suspicious. She was also flattered that he'd evidently noticed her at school, though she hoped he didn't read too much into the claim that she talked about him at home. She'd never live it down if the rumour spread that Darcie Lock had a crush on Kassim al Yaqoubi. There was enough to worry about without that added embarrassment.

On the other hand, he was really nice.

Once safely hidden behind an arrangement of gaudy blooms, Doreen heaved a sigh. 'Phew! That was way harder than I thought.' She grabbed a glass of champagne from a passing waitress and downed it in three gulps. 'Right, Darcie, back into the fray. I'll tackle Madame Tsui. Stay in sight so she can see your lovely new dress – she'll be interested in that.'

'It's one of hers, you know,' said Darcie, relieved to be let off being present during the humiliation of begging another supper.

'Wow!' Doreen had a better idea than Darcie as to how many dollars that represented. 'However did your mom afford it?'

Darcie was about to say something but her companion saved her the trouble, putting a finger on her lips.

'No, don't tell me. I bet she hasn't let on to your dad, has she? My, won't he have a heart attack when he sees the next Amex bill.'

Doreen sallied off into the crowd milling around the lawn, leaving Darcie sincerely hoping that her dad would be there to open his bank statement.

The second approach did not go so well. Darcie could see Doreen was meeting quiet but firm refusals from Madame Tsui while two nervous bodyguards looked on. They did not know quite what to make of this brash American verbally assaulting the fortress of their employer's reserve.

'My aunt will never allow me to invite anyone back to her place.'

Darcie jumped. Pearl Cheng was standing at her shoulder, watching the scene unfold. She was dressed in another of Madame Tsui's creations, this one in vivid blues and green.

'I don't know why you want to come in any case,' Pearl continued bluntly. 'We're not really friends, are we? Perhaps you're just like the other girls, hoping for a few free samples?'

'No. I'm not really interested in clothes,' Darcie replied, wondering what had made the girl so cynical.

'That's what I thought, until I saw you this afternoon. That's this season's, isn't it?' She nodded down at the dress.

'I wouldn't know. It's a present.'

'Oh.' Pearl was losing interest. Her gaze drifted away over the crowd. Darcie studied her surreptitiously. Pearl was perfect, from her slim figure to her glossy black hair. Yet when the girl turned to face her, Darcie saw that her dark almond-shaped eyes were sad. 'Don't try to come round, Darcie. Nice girls like you wouldn't like it.'

'Why not?'

'You wouldn't understand.'

Darcie caught Pearl's arm before she could move away. She'd forgotten all about her mission; she just wanted to reach this girl who seemed even lonelier than her. 'Try me. I'd like to be a friend if I can.'

Pearl smiled bitterly. 'I don't have friends. I'm not allowed.' She firmly disengaged her arm from Darcie's grasp and disappeared back into the crowd.

The steady beat of a marching band drew everyone's attention from their conversations. A flash of scarlet, black and white appeared round the corner of the residence. A soldier at the front tossed his stick in the air, catching it deftly as it twirled to earth. A ripple of appreciation passed through the crowd.

'Hey, Darcie.' A heavy arm draped over her shoulders. It was attached to target number three: Hugo Kraus. 'Do you go in for this stuff, military bands and all that?'

Darcie wasn't sure what to do. Her shoulders didn't want to give this creep house room. Could she pull away without offending him? 'Be nice' had been her orders.

'Not really my scene. Would you like a drink?' She

used this as an excuse to make a move towards the table, ducking out from under his arm.

'Sure. Anything.' He smiled at her as she handed him a fruit juice. 'Great dress.'

'Thanks. It's a Tsui.'

'Really? I'm impressed.' He took another step towards her, arm once more resting on her shoulders.

Perhaps that's why he has so many girlfriends, Darcie thought to herself: he's too lazy to stand on his own feet.

'Shall we go somewhere quieter, away from the bagpipes?' he asked, breathing heavily over her. Though he had classic good looks, even down to the sparkling blue eyes and square jaw, Darcie found him cold.

'Actually, I'm prepared to have my musical taste expanded today,' Darcie said, nodding over to the band.

'Go for men in skirts, do you?' He brushed his fingers against her bare back. She moved away quickly.

They were preferable to snakes in chinos, but she kept this thought to herself and merely smiled.

Hugo linked her arm in his. 'Come on then, Darcie, let's see the Highlanders fling.'

The party ended at dusk. Darcie was relieved to return to the sanctuary of her room, away from the attentions of Hugo Kraus. It had been too easy to get an invitation to his place – 'Next weekend, a little gathering of friends out on the ranch, you must come, Darcie. Pick you up at the Stanley.' He was certainly interested in her – but whether the interest was the kind Gladys had warned her to look out for or stemmed from the fact that she was one of the few girls in school he had yet to go out with, Darcie didn't know. He collected girlfriends like white hunters used to collect big game trophies. She wouldn't be surprised if he had mugshots of his past conquests lined up on the wall of his bedroom all grinning adoringly at him.

She took a quick shower in her private bathroom and put on her pyjamas, thinking about the homework she still had to do. Toothbrush in hand, she wandered into the bedroom in search of her schoolbag. She stopped. A tall black Highlander was bent over her dressing table, a set of bagpipes crumpled on the bed like an antelope that had been hit by a lorry, legs stuck out at strange angles. She nearly laughed.

'Um, hi, I'm afraid you must have taken a wrong turn,' she said pleasantly, waving her toothbrush towards the door.

The soldier turned round. With the heightened awareness that comes with a rush of adrenalin, Darcie noticed that he had a heavy gold bracelet dangling on his wrist and the contents of her make-up bag were scattered everywhere.

She backed towards the bathroom. 'You'd better get out or I'll call someone,' she threatened, trying to sound more confident than she felt.

She missed the moment when everything changed. Suddenly, the man had crossed the room, caught her by the arms, forced her face down on to the bed, her scream muffled in the duvet. From the weight pressing on her back, he must be kneeling on her. She couldn't breathe. One hand was released but, before she could do anything, she felt a ring of cold steel pushed into the nape of her neck.

'Scream again and I'll shoot,' the man hissed.

Darcie stopped thrashing and lay still, shifting just enough to free her mouth and nose so that she didn't suffocate. None of Gladys's lessons had prepared her for this. She'd never said anything about being smothered in the high commissioner's residence.

'Easy now, sister. My employer wants something he gave your dear papa. We know you have it.' The man was calm but Darcie had no doubt he meant to kill her if she made a move.

'I don't have anything. Where's my father? What have you done with him?' she asked desperately.

The gun pressed harder into her flesh as the man shifted his weight. He seemed to be listening to something outside. She could hear it too. There were shouts and doors banging. The fire alarm went off in the corridor.

'Seems we do not have long, sister,' the man said.

'Why not be kind to yourself and hand it over, *sawa*?'

'Hand what over?' Darcie felt numb. Would he just shoot her when he realised this was a waste of time?

'Do not be clever with me. Lock had a disk belonging to my employer. He told us he gave it to you. He said you and the disk would be out of the country by now. It was our lucky day when we found you had stayed. My employer wants it back and he wants it now.'

'I don't know what you're talking about.' The man pressed the gun harder into her neck.

Suddenly the door to the bedroom burst open. A soldier stood framed in the doorway. He was still dressed in his ceremonial best but now carrying a rather more offensive weapon than a musical instrument. He trained the rifle on Darcie's assailant. For a split second, her attacker lessened the pressure of the gun on her neck to check behind him. Darcie grabbed for the first object at hand – the bagpipes – and hefted them over her shoulder. The pipes whacked her assailant in the face. In the confusion as he wrestled them away, she slid out from under him and got as far as the floor. He made a lunge for her hair. Now a shot rang out. A second shot and a man screamed. The soldier fell back into the corridor.

'Man down, man down!' Voices and feet echoed outside. Shadows passed the windows at a run.

Darcie was dragged to her feet by her hair, the gun back at her neck, but this time her attacker was standing behind her, using her as a shield.

'In here!' Darcie yelled before the barrel dug painfully into her throat.

'Shut up or you die!'

'Hostage situation – we have, I repeat, a hostage situation,' boomed a voice in the corridor. An eerie stillness fell as everyone waited for more orders. Darcie could hear her own heart pounding, smell the sweat running off her captor, feel the heat of his breath on her neck.

'We are coming out!' Darcie's attacker shouted. 'No one try anything or I shoot the girl.'

Half carrying, half dragging, he shoved her out into

the hallway. The injured soldier had pulled himself against a wall; he was bleeding from a leg wound on to the white carpet. At least three more soldiers had the pair in the sights of their rifles.

'Step away from the girl and give yourself up!' called out an officer. Darcie could see him sheltering by the door into the dining room.

The man laughed and tightened his grip. 'You are joking, man. Anyone moves and she dies. Hey, brother!' He nodded at the soldier crouched by the entrance. 'Open the door.'

The officer nodded and the soldier shoved the front doors apart.

'Now, stay back while we go for a little walk.' The man pushed Darcie forward, marching her towards the front entrance and out into the night. Carpet and marble was replaced by gravel. Darcie yelped as stones dug into her bare feet, earning her a blow from the fist holding the gun.

'Shut up!' he growled, head darting left and right as he watched for any attempts to rescue her.

Darcie's mind was racing. She was surprised at how clearly she could think – terrified though she was, she felt focused, knowing her survival depended on making the right choices. One thing was clear: if she left with him she'd probably be dead before the morning.

'Please let me go,' she pleaded as he hurried her down the drive. Soldiers followed taking cover in the bushes on all sides, but they were powerless to stop what was going on. 'You don't need me. I don't have what you came for. I really don't.'

'*Pole sana*, sister, but we do need you. I was told if I could not find the disk then I should persuade you to come with me. We think having you around might help Papa remember just what he did with it.' He paused at the end of the drive. The gates were shut but a white Land Cruiser raced out of the shadows and drew up on the opposite side of the road. 'Open the gate!' he shouted.

With an electric hum, they swung open. There were only a few metres left between them and the car. Pity she wasn't wearing shoes. Barefoot she wasn't sure this was going to work.

'I think I'm going to be sick,' Darcie gasped, faking a retch.

The man glanced down at her; momentarily his grip loosened as he held her away from his body.

That was enough. Darcie planted a kick to his shin, simultaneously swivelling round to bite the soft skin between thumb and finger on the hand gripping her. A gun fired. Her ears rang with the report and she felt a scorching pain on her shoulder. She twisted again to knee him in the groin. A grunt and his grasp weakened. She ducked down, escaping his arms. A hand made a grab for her but the silky material of her pyjamas slipped clear. He cursed, taking another swipe but she was already running. More shots exploded around them as the soldiers opened fire. She threw herself flat, afraid of being caught in the crossfire. A body landed on top of her and she had a moment's panic until she realised it was a soldier trying to protect her. Lying very still, she listened to the crackle of guns and the screech of tyres as a vehicle pulled away at high speed.

Finally, the soldier picked himself up off Darcie.

'You all right, miss?' he asked, helping her to her feet. It was just her luck that the nearest soldier had been the giant who wielded the bass drum.

'A bit shaken,' Darcie admitted with a feeble attempt at a smile. She was trembling, bruised, and her shoulder was aching. 'I think I'll just sit down again.' Before I fall down, she might have added.

'Easy, miss. It's all over now.'

More soldiers had reached them, one carrying a medical kit. 'Are you hurt, lassie?' the medic asked.

'Shoulder,' said Darcie, putting her head on her knees. He lifted her chin gently and eased her back on the ground.

'Ah, it's just a wee nick. Not much to write home about.' He dressed it swiftly, talking to her all the time to stop her passing out on him. 'If my other patient told the truth, those flying bagpipes make a better tale for your mam. Now, get her into the house.' The last remark was directed to the bass drummer. Darcie was lifted off the floor and carried back the way she had so recently been dragged.

'Did you catch him?' she asked hoarsely, her eyes closed. She could hear the medic walking alongside her.

'Nay, lass. Just winged him. But don't fret – he's gone. Stay with us, won't you, lassie?'

'I'll try. Any one else hurt?'

'Private Maclaren – the soldier who found you first – and Sergeant Gordon – the unwilling donor of the uniform. He was jumped in the gents, poor sod, and now he'll never see his gear again. Lump on his head like a goose's egg.'

Re-entering the bright lights of the residence, Darcie opened her eyes briefly. The faces of Sir Stephen and Lady Graham swum in and out of focus, behind them a grim Gladys Smith.

'Is she all right?' the high commissioner demanded.

'Yes, sir,' reported the medic. 'Took a slight flesh wound when she escaped her attacker – nothing serious. She was a real hero, this wee lass. Would have been bundled in that car before we could do anything for her if she hadn't taken a risk.'

Her Majesty's representative to Kenya swore under his breath. 'Better take her back to her room.'

'We'll put a guard on the residence tonight in addition to your usual arrangements, sir,' said the commanding officer, coming to join the group in the foyer. 'Damn bold burglars you have here, if you don't mind me saying, though I doubt that one will come back for more.'

Darcie was carried to her bed, her ears still ringing from the gunshot. The medic checked her wound again and replaced his temporary dressing with a proper bandage.

'There, lass, you can rest now. I'm not worried about you fainting on me. Hardly any blood lost – just a graze and a scorch mark from the gun. He must have fired it close to your skin but the bullet passed over your shoulder. I've seen worse.'

Darcie eased herself up into a sitting position. Her head was thumping but she had to tell someone her news. 'Can I see Gladys Smith? She's outside.'

The medic sucked his teeth. 'Just for a moment. I'll come back and check on you in twenty minutes. And when I do I want to find you in bed and asleep. That's an order.'

'Yes, sir,' Darcie said with a faint smile. 'Thank you.'

Gladys appeared at her side. 'What is it, Darcie?'

'Dad's alive,' she said. 'He's still alive.'

8

07.30, Nairobi: Storms easing overnight, leaving a scattering of showers.

Darcie's breakfast arrived the next morning on a tray – a fresh roll nestling in a folded napkin, a curl of butter, and miniature pots of honey and jam. It felt like being in a top-class hotel. The only unusual item was a white envelope leaning against the silver teapot. Ignoring the food, Darcie opened it and out fell an airline ticket to Washington for a flight leaving that evening. One-way. Dumping the tray, she threw back the covers and swung her legs out of bed. They weren't going to send her to the States now, not when she knew her dad still had a chance.

The corridor outside her room was empty. A new arrangement of orange bird-of-paradise flowers had appeared on the hall table. The white carpet had been removed and all signs of the struggle eliminated. She went in search of Sir Stephen, guessing he might still be at breakfast. A raised voice from the dining room alerted Darcie to the presence of the high commissioner before she even opened the door.

'Absolutely not. I refuse to allow her to stay another day, let alone another week! Isn't it enough you almost got her killed last night? We can't take risks now – we've got more than enough on our plate with the security issues surrounding the polo tournament. The prince was supposed to be staying here. What will the Palace say when they find out that guests have been attacked in their bedrooms?'

'That's not my concern, Stephen.' Gladys was talking in her most icy tone of voice. 'Where the junior royals spend their holidays is nothing to do with me. I have a job to get on with.'

'Well it should be your concern! How on earth did that man get in here in the first place?'

'According to the CCTV, it seems he came in with the entourage surrounding the minister for trade. The minister's office claim they know nothing about him, of course.'

'That isn't good enough. You've got to wrap this up now, Gladys. Clear the mess up before the weekend.' Darcie held her breath. The 'mess' was her dad. She wasn't going to let anyone give up on him now; and she hoped Gladys wouldn't either.

'May I remind you, Stephen, that this operation is not under your control? I am head of station here and am acting under orders from my superior. The minister herself has authorised our department to carry out the investigation.' Darcie silently applauded Agent Smith's firm tone.

'I bet the minister would feel differently about that if she learnt what happened yesterday. You promised me the girl would be in no danger – just asking a few questions, nothing more. Next thing I know, some thug gatecrashes the QBP and shoots the place up in an attempt to kidnap a fourteen-year-old girl placed in my care. It's pure madness to continue.'

'Madness to want to save Michael? Madness to want to expose the traffickers? It's more than just Darcie's life we're discussing here, Stephen. Besides, I thought she handled herself very well last night. Don't you?'

'I know that, but what you're proposing is completely unethical. Letting her continue when we know there are people wanting to use her to make Michael talk – surely even you can see that the best thing is to get her as far away from here as possible?'

'I disagree. If we do that, we'll have signed Michael's death certificate. While Darcie is here – while they think she has this disk they're after – there's still a chance for him.'

'But she's a teenager, for pity's sake!'

'This is a war, Stephen. You have to take risks.'

'What war?'

'The war on terror. You know as well as I do that the smuggling operation is keeping the East African terrorist network alive. Without it, the cells will wither on the vine.'

'All right – call it a war if you want. But even wars have rules under international law – a ban on the use of child combatants being one of them.'

'She is not a combatant.'

'So don't put her in the line of fire – put her on a plane home.'

Darcie decided she'd heard enough. The argument had reached stalemate. She pushed the door open and walked in. She'd expected to find just Gladys and Sir Stephen; instead she found a gathering of most of the senior staff of the High Commission seated around the gleaming dining room table. The room fell silent as everyone turned to look at her. She wished she had thought to get dressed – pale blue pyjamas and slippers did not create the right impression for what she wanted to say.

'Oh, um, good morning, Darcie,' said the high commissioner lamely. 'Did you sleep well?'

'Yes, thank you.' She might as well grab the bull by the horns: 'I want to stay.'

'What's that?'

'I was listening just now to the . . . er . . . discussion. I can't leave when I know Dad's alive. I know you don't want me here; I know it's dangerous, but I want to see this through.' Sir Stephen looked down at his file of papers, avoiding her eye. Darcie continued, 'I'm sorry if I'm causing difficulties for your other guests – I'll go somewhere else if you want, get out of the way – but I want to stay in Nairobi.'

'You can't possibly understand what you are getting yourself into, Darcie,' he said heavily.

'I know you want the best for me, sir, but it's my dad we're talking about. I have the right to make my own decision.'

Sir Stephen seemed on the point of disputing this but he was interrupted.

'May I say something?' It was Major Parker, the defence attaché and Darcie's fencing teacher.

The high commissioner looked up in hope of some support for his view. 'Go ahead, major.'

'I know Darcie: we've spent a lot of time together at the club. She's a level-headed girl who won't take unnecessary risks. If you lay down the conditions on which you'd be prepared to allow her to stay, I'm sure she'll keep to them.'

Darcie felt a wave of gratitude for her tutor. It was the first time she'd heard such praise from him. He'd never shown any sign that he rated her abilities when they'd been fencing.

'As for a place to stay while the prince is here, my wife and I would be more than happy to host her.'

The high commissioner sighed and put his head in his hands.

'That won't be necessary, major. Other views?' he asked wearily.

Ben cleared his throat. 'We can keep her under surveillance the whole time she's here, sir. We'll line up a bodyguard for the trip to and from school and to any other place she visits. I can arrange to have an SAS team on standby to bring her out at a moment's notice. They're already here at the villa for their briefing on plans for Michael Lock's rescue – when we find him, that is. I'm sure their commander can identify one of them to act as her close personal protection. Oh, and the CIA will want to help too.'

'Not the Americans,' groaned Sir Stephen.

'Yes, sir. I'm afraid so. Their signals' intelligence is much better than ours. They'll be listening in to every conversation in Nairobi searching for relevant hits. Any mention of Michael or Darcie and we'll be there.'

The high commissioner folded his hands together. 'I can see that I'm going to have to bow to the inevitable. I can't overrule our colleagues here; all I can do, it seems, is lay down a few conditions. So be it. I insist that you pull Darcie out at the first sign of trouble. Don't risk her a minute longer than strictly necessary just to see if she turns up more leads. Do I make myself clear?'

'Yes, Stephen,' agreed Gladys. 'All we need is a hint of the whereabouts of Michael, then we can do the rest.'

'I'll hold you to that. And Darcie?'

'Yes?' Darcie had been looking at her slippers for the past few minutes while she listened to the discussion going on over her head.

Sir Stephen gave a deep sigh. 'Hadn't you better get ready for school?'

*

Darcie hadn't forgotten the disk. As she dressed, she wondered if her dad had made up the story, believing she was thousands of miles away, using her as cover to hide what he'd really done with it. Or maybe it was the truth? She had a big collection of CDs – it was possible he may have concealed something among them, knowing it was unlikely she'd come across it before he took it back. But why would he do that? Surely he would have kept something like that at work. Well, there was only one way to find out. Where were her CDs now? Boxed up and waiting to be shipped out? She must ask Gladys or Ben to get them for her if they hadn't thought of this already.

Joel the driver was not alone in the front of the red Jag when Darcie slid into the back. She'd been promised a bodyguard and here he was. The man's thick neck, broken nose and scar running down his left cheek made his profession all too apparent.

'Morning,' said Darcie.

The bodyguard grunted.

'Morning, miss,' replied Joel brightly. 'Running a bit late today?'

'Had a rough night.'

'So I heard, miss. I'm pleased to see you up and about today.'

'Thank you. I'm Darcie Lock by the way.' She directed this to the other man.

'Warrant Officer Galt.'

'I'm impressed,' admitted Darcie. She'd forgotten that Ben had mentioned the SAS; this must be one of them. 'When I heard I was to get a bodyguard, I was half expecting a bouncer from the Safari Club; I didn't know I was getting a military escort,' she joked. He made no response. 'I won't worry now I've got you.'

'I don't know about that,' said Warrant Officer Galt, adjusting the wing mirror. 'If I were you, I'd worry that they thought you might need me.' She had to admit he had a point. 'Kids shouldn't be mixed up in this business.'

His short hair seemed to bristle with indignation; his neck was flushed pink. Darcie guessed he'd just had a blazing row with his superior about this assignment but that was hardly her fault.

'I didn't want to get involved. It just happened,' she said, stuffing her football boots into her new sports bag. They were a bit muddy but she hadn't had time to sort them out.

'No, I don't suppose you did, Miss Lock.' He paused. 'You know, you really should clean your kit.'

The car turned out on to the main road. Darcie looked up from the bag and saw Warrant Officer Galt studying her in the mirror. His boxer's face broke into a slow smile when their eyes met.

'Sorry, sir, but I've been a bit busy stopping myself being killed,' she said acerbically.

'My commanding officer would never accept that excuse.'

'Well, I don't have a commanding officer.'

'What about the old silver dragon?'

'Yeah, well.' Darcie flicked the mud off her knee on to the spotless floor of the Jag, then felt bad about doing so. She hoped Joel hadn't noticed.

'Did you really fight that punk off with bagpipes?' the soldier asked with a grin. He'd seen her guilty expression in his mirror.

Darcie shrugged and returned his smile, pleased to find that Galt had a human side after all. 'They did get dragged in to it, yes.'

He gave a whistle. 'I'll have to tell the lads. They never thought to mention that during training. They've missed a trick there.'

'Still, I bet they didn't mention that you'd end up doing the school run either, did they?'

His smile broadened, displaying a couple of gold teeth. 'You're right there, miss.'

'Call me Darcie.'

'OK, Darcie. As I'm babysitter for the week, you'd better call me Stingo.'

'OK, Stingo.'

Joel chuckled. 'Next you're going to ask him why he's called that. I tell you, miss, it ain't no story for a lady's ears.'

'Right,' said Darcie warily. 'Perhaps we'll leave that

till we know each other better then. I'm in for a tough morning as it is.'

'Why's that?' asked Stingo, his attention back on the road as he scanned the other vehicles for any concealed threat to his charge.

'Homework. Second time I haven't done it this week. I'm in big trouble.'

Mrs Pringle asked Darcie to stay behind after class.

'So, Darcie, you expect me to believe that you were attacked last night by a burglar in a kilt, shot at, and then flattened by a bass drummer from the Highland band?'

'Yes, Mrs Pringle.'

'As an excuse, it has the merit of being more inventive than the average, but you can understand if I fail to follow you on your little flight of fantasy.'

Mrs Pringle was striding to and fro in front of the white board. Darcie was standing sheepishly by the teacher's desk. She knew her explanation had been doomed the moment she'd opened her mouth.

No wonder spies told lies – it was far easier than the alternative.

'But it's the truth, miss.'

'Even if half what you tell me bears any connection to reality, Darcie, it still doesn't get your homework done. I let you off once because of the unfortunate family circumstances, but I would be doing you no favours if I did so again. You will stay behind after school. I promise to find you a room free of mad bagpipers so you can catch up.'

'But, miss, I'm supposed to be going to Kassim's tonight.'

'Then you'll be late. You can tell the Yaqoubis why – if you dare.'

Darcie contemplated ringing the High Commission to get someone to verify her story, but quickly decided against it. If she was to make discreet enquiries about her father, she didn't want to start colourful stories about her circulating all over the school. And as Mrs Pringle had made clear, even if she was telling the truth, she was still dropping behind with her work.

'OK, miss. I'll stay behind tonight and catch up.'

Mrs Pringle kept her word and found Darcie a vacant classroom next to the staffroom.

'Here you are. Not a flash of tartan in sight. Knock on the hatch when you've finished,' the teacher said primly, carrying off a pile of marking.

Darcie had only managed to solve two problems when the door opened and Stingo burst into the room.

'What the hell you playing at?' he shouted at her. 'You're my responsibility after school hours. Don't do that again!'

She had completely forgotten her guard of honour. From the SAS man's agitated manner, he'd obviously watched the students leave, noticed she was missing, and drawn a dire conclusion.

'I'm sorry. I'm in detention,' said Darcie, gesturing to the textbooks.

This did nothing to calm him.

'What you go and get detention for?' He put his face close to hers and hissed, 'I thought you were supposed to be going to the Yaqoubi place, or has that plan changed too without anyone feeling the need to tell me?'

'No, I'm still going. I'll just have to be late, that's all. Kassim knows I've been made to stay behind.'

'Hell, Darcie, I thought you were smart. You don't mess with this kind of work. You're going to get us all killed if you carry on like this.'

That was so unfair.

'You're not helping, Stingo. You're supposed to be protecting, not nagging me. I have to act normal, remember, and try to forget I was shot at yesterday and my dad's held by a bunch of killers.' She could feel her anger getting the better of her; she gritted her teeth to keep a lid on it. 'And in my case, being normal includes detention. So unless you're any good at maths, I suggest you shut up and let me finish this.'

Stingo stamped out of the room again, swearing under his breath.

The Yaqoubi villa was set in its own grounds in one of the most exclusive neighbourhoods in Nairobi.

The estate was an old colonial farm that had been swallowed by the city, but it still retained its paddocks and outbuildings. The family didn't encourage visitors for it was surrounded by a high white wall bristling with surveillance cameras. The sun was low in the sky by the time the cherry red Jag reached the gate. Lean shadows of trees stretched across the private road. Three Hadada ibis, their grey wings glistening with a metallic sheen, fluttered down to land on the verge, rooting out insects with their long, curved beaks. Their raucous cries splintered the evening calm, following the car as it turned into the estate.

'How big is this place?' Darcie asked Joel as they drove down the driveway leading to the house. Darcie knew the high commissioner had insisted his driver accompany her because Joel was the most highly trained driver on the staff, skilled at evasion should another kidnap attempt be made.

Joel gave a rich laugh. 'Look on the map, miss, and you see it is very big. Mr Yaqoubi must be a very rich man. They tell me he has stables stocked with the finest Arabian horses. You should ask to see them.'

Stingo was still sulking in the front seat.

'What are you going to do while I'm in there?' Darcie asked her bodyguard.

'Finish your homework for you, I suppose,' he grumbled. 'Stop you getting any more detentions.'

'Great. I didn't know you could read,' she teased

'Watch it, Darcie. I've been trained to kill with my bare hands.'

'So, when you've read and summarised chapter eight of *Great Expectations*, what then?'

'What you think, you muppet? I'll be sticking with Joel and the car, listening in on the mike. If I hear you in trouble, I'll be there.'

Darcie nervously patted the microphone concealed in her hairband.

'Don't do that!' swore Stingo. 'It sounds like thunder right in my ear. It's a very sensitive bit of kit.'

'And I thought you SAS types were supposed to be tough,' Darcie said accusingly as she got out of the car.

A white-robed servant opened the door and ushered

her into the hallway. As Darcie moved through the house in his wake, she felt she'd stepped out of Africa and into Arabia. Intricate carved screens decorated the windows casting the rooms into half-light; Persian rugs in sumptuous colours stretched before low chairs; the air smelt of sandalwood.

'Come, come,' said the servant, beckoning her forward. He opened the last door at the end of a passage, revealing a room scattered with bright plastic toys and two girls of about seven wrestling on the floor. The twins stopped mid-tumble and turned to look at the visitor.

'It's her!' the one with long plaits whispered loudly. They sprang apart and stood looking up at her demurely.

'Welcome to our house,' the second girl announced formally. Apart from having her hair in a ponytail, she looked just like her sister. 'I'm Ali and this is Kari. Mama said you've come to play with us.'

'Oh.' Darcie was taken aback. The Yaqoubis had obviously taken Doreen at her word. That was the last thing she had expected. As an only child with no relatives, she had no experience playing with younger children. 'Well then, what do you want to play?' She looked round the room for inspiration. 'Shall we get out your dolls?'

'No, that's boring,' announced Ali.

'Drawing?'

'Yawn, yawn, yawn,' commented Kari. She looked around for something to kick, found her sister and a new scuffle broke out.

'I know,' said Darcie desperately. She seized a ball from the top of the cupboard. 'I'll teach you to play football.'

Yells of approval met this suggestion and the girls threw open the French windows and led her down on to the lawn.

Darcie laid out a goal against the house wall. 'Ali –'

'I'm Kari.'

Darcie grinned. 'No you're not. Ali, you be in goal. Kari and I will try and score. After five minutes, we'll all swap round. Now, Kari, do you know how to kick a ball?'

'Ple-ease!' said Kari, rolling her eyes in a way that made her look far older than her seven years.

'Don't give me that. I'm not talking about whether you touch it or not, but what part of the foot you use, how you control it, that kind of thing.'

Kari stopped looking like a sulky mini-teenager and began to pay close attention as Darcie showed her a few basic techniques.

'I've got it!' Kari announced confidently after a few minutes. 'Let me try now!'

The twins were enthusiastic rather than accurate with their shooting. Darcie spent most of her time digging through the shrubs looking for the ball and on one occasion only narrowly saved a window from an exuberant kick.

'See, I did it!' shouted Kari. 'I kicked it with the side of my foot, I really did.'

Darcie didn't like to point out that the idea was to gain more, rather than less control, over the ball. The girls were so clearly enjoying themselves. Even Darcie had forgotten what she was here for when a fourth player wearing jodhpurs joined the team. Kassim swooped in, picked up Kari, ran the length of the lawn with her, stole the ball off Ali and took a shot at goal. Darcie dived but it brushed her fingertips and hit the wall behind her.

'Goal!' shouted Kassim, grabbing Ali under his other arm and dancing like a lunatic round the pitch with his sisters.

Darcie picked herself up. Her white school shirt was now a wreck.

'Let the zebra have a go!' squealed Kari excitedly.

'Who's zebra?' Darcie asked, looking round with a frown.

'I'm afraid they mean you. Forgive my sisters, they are brutes,' said Kassim, tweaking Kari by the nose.

Darcie touched her face self-consciously: both it and her shirt were streaked with mud from her enthusiastic dive into the shrubbery.

'Oman one, England nil.' Kassim ran to take her place in the goal. 'Let's see if she is as rubbish as her countrymen at taking a penalty.'

Mucking about with the twins was one thing, playing against Kassim, the best footballer in the school, was another. Darcie felt her confidence ebbing away even as she ran up to kick. It was a lousy strike, sailing straight towards him. He grinned and deflected it easily. As the ball flew towards her, her reflexes took over. She leapt and headed it into the corner of the goal. It was only as her hairband dug into her scalp that she realised she had given Stingo something rather more substantial to complain about.

Two mini torpedoes struck her side on, knocking her to the grass. 'Girls, one! Girls, one!' the twins chanted.

'Ali, Kari!' boomed a man's voice from the veranda. 'Get off our guest immediately!'

The girls sprung to their feet at once, looking scared. Kassim hung his head and began dribbling the ball away as if he had had nothing to do with any of it.

'Inside, both of you. Your mother wants you. It's time you were in bed.' Mr Yaqoubi stood with a phone in one hand and a sheaf of papers in the other.

'Yes, Abu,' intoned the twins.

Darcie wondered if she was in trouble for encouraging such unladylike behaviour but if she was, Mr Yaqoubi did not display his annoyance.

'Kassim, why don't you show our guest around before we eat? I still have work to do and your mother is busy.'

'Yes, Abu. Come on, Darcie, I'll take you to the stables.'

'Sorry about that,' muttered Darcie when she'd caught up with him. She rubbed her face on her arm, painfully aware that she must look a sight.

'Sorry about what?'

'Getting your sisters all stirred up and everything.'

'Oh, don't mind them,' Kassim said as he tapped in a security code to the stable block door. 'They're pretty stirred up most of the time. I'm sorry I wasn't here to meet you. I didn't hear you arrive.'

He led Darcie into a covered arena that smelt of sawdust and horse. Under the bright lights, two stable boys were exercising a couple of ponies.

'I thought you had Arabians,' said Darcie.

'We do. These are my polo ponies – Abu got them

for me from Argentina. Pure bred Ciollos. I'm very proud of them.' Kassim stepped forward and took the reins of the nearest from the stable boy. 'Do you ride?'

'Yes,' said Darcie warily. The pony had given her a sly look almost as if it understood the question. 'But I've never played polo.'

'Haven't you? I think I even prefer it to football.'

'Are you any good?'

Kassim shrugged modestly. 'Not really. But I am on the Country Club team. I'll be playing a tournament this Sunday.'

'So you're not that bad either.'

'I suppose not. Do you want to have a go? I'll teach you.'

'OK. Don't expect much though.'

'Of course not. You're just a girl after all.'

He was teasing her again, but the challenge was clear. Darcie grimaced at him and selected a mallet from the rack along the wall.

'What do I do with this? Hit you on the head until you learn not to make such sexist comments?'

'Alternatively, you could try and hit the ball – side on, not with the end.' He passed her a helmet, another trial for the listening Stingo to endure.

She mounted the pony, waiting while Kassim shortened the stirrups for her.

'What's his name?' she asked, patting the pony on the neck.

'Loco.'

Lunatic. That followed.

'Take him for a trot round the ring. Rest your mallet on your shoulder ready to swing down at the target. Keep it loose. Relax.'

'I'm trying,' Darcie shouted. It was taking all her concentration to keep the wilful pony under control.

Kassim appeared at her side on another mount with a rough chestnut coat. If a pony could look smug, then this one did.

'Why not take a swing at the ball?' he asked.

'Here goes nothing.' Darcie urged the pony towards the white target, a little bigger than a tennis ball, lying on the dirt. As she approached, she leant over Loco's shoulder and struck. Her mallet passed straight over the top of it.

'Bad luck!' called Kassim. He followed in her tracks, took a swipe and the ball sailed sweetly into the air with a resounding crack.

'Show off,' muttered Darcie. Kassim grinned at her, obviously enjoying the chance to display his skills.

She cantered after the ball, took aim and struck. This time she made contact and it flew into the air – only to hit one of the stable boys in the stomach. So much for control over balls.

'Oh no! I'm so sorry,' said Darcie. She dismounted quickly and ran over to her victim. She would have sworn that Stingo was chuckling away as he listened in to the fiasco. 'Are you all right?'

'Yes, miss. No problem,' panted the man. 'It happens all the time.'

Kassim was roaring with laughter behind her. 'Next lesson is to learn to direct the ball at the goal rather than the spectators, Darcie,' he said.

He seemed to enjoy watching her humiliating

herself, but Darcie had had enough lessons. All this exercise reminded her that her shoulder was still sore from yesterday. 'Thanks but no thanks – that's it for me. I don't think I'd better chance my luck.'

She handed the reins for her pony to one of the stable boys and began to walk away. Kassim swung out of his saddle and hastened after her.

'Sorry, Darcie, I shouldn't have laughed. Are you all right?' He noticed that she'd been flexing her injured shoulder. He put a hand briefly on her arm but then let it drop.

'You should be asking your stable boy that, not me. He was the one who got hit.'

'But your shoulder?' His concern appeared genuine. Darcie was flattered.

'Really, Kassim, it's nothing, just a bit stiff. Look, why don't you stay and carry on with your practice?' She nodded over to the waiting ponies.

He was easily persuadable: he had not been joking when he said polo was his first love. 'OK. But you mustn't go wandering off on your own – the dogs will be loose in the grounds now and they'll eat you for supper if they find you. Why don't you take a shower and get ready for dinner? There's changing rooms over there. Come back and watch when you're ready.'

'OK. Would someone fetch my bag from the car for me?'

Kassim gave a whistle and the injured stable boy limped over.

'Miss Lock's bag, please. Take it to the changing rooms.'

Darcie pressed the tag on her bag and unzipped. She guessed she had around fifteen minutes before Kassim would wonder what had become of her – enough time to do some snooping. Her little black dress was about to go on its first outing.

But what about the dogs? She slipped the can of pepper spray into her belt, wondering if it would work on animals. Knowing her luck it would just make them more irate. But the chance to scout around and see if her father was imprisoned somewhere close by could not be passed up. If he were here it was unlikely that he would be kept in the house near the family, but the outbuildings around the stable block – they were another matter entirely.

The crack of mallet on ball indicated that Kassim was happily employed in the arena. She felt a momentary temptation to go back and join him. For all the humiliation, it had been fun being with him. They'd got on so easily, teasing each other like old friends. No, that had to wait – her dad came first. She slipped quietly out into the yard. Loose boxes made up three sides of the square. Each had a name nailed over the door – Saladin, Luxor, Desert Rose – presumably the homes of the famous Arabian horses. Keeping to the shadows, she peered over the top of the first and almost screamed as a dark shape loomed towards her, butting her gently with its nose. It was only a magnificent black mare in search of a treat. Darcie gulped and cursed her stupidity. She fondled the soft skin just above the nostrils and moved on.

The Yaqoubi collection of racehorses was impressive. Darcie guessed that a single one of them would cost far more money than her parents had ever earned in a year and Kassim's father had at least fifteen of these beauties. More disappointing was the fact that there was no suspicious locked door, no sound of any human inhabitants. She'd have to look further afield.

She let herself out of the stable block and headed through the trees for the nearest set of buildings. Fireflies flickered in the darkness, the cicadas were playing their grating tune at full volume. She stumbled several times over roots as she ran. She really needed a torch but there was no time to go back to find one. As she approached the sheds, she could hear barking ahead. The dogs were very excited, but not about her. That was a relief: she didn't fancy her chances against them. She was about to turn and search elsewhere while they were occupied when she heard a familiar voice swearing.

Stingo.

Reluctantly, she ran towards the commotion. Reaching the corner of the outhouse, she saw him backed up against a garage door, using a rake to keep two Alsatians at bay.

'Idiot!' muttered Darcie. Looking around, she grabbed a fire extinguisher fixed to the wall, wrenched the nozzle free and pressed the pump. Foam cascaded all over the dogs and Stingo. Paws slipped. Barks became yelps.

'Run!' she shouted, setting the example by dashing towards the stables.

Stingo caught up with her, covered in white suds. He was first through the door Darcie had left wedged open, waited for her to clear it, then slammed it shut. Claws skittered on the other side. Howls and barks rent the air.

'Quick, in here,' said Darcie, dragging Stingo into the ladies' changing room. Feet pounded along the corridor outside. Floodlights switched on all round the building. 'What were you playing at?' she asked him angrily, hands on her hips as he collapsed on the bench. 'I thought you said you were going to wait in the car?'

Stingo glared at her, wiping foam from his eyes. 'No point. Couldn't hear a thing, thanks to your antics on the football pitch. My head's still ringing.'

'So you got bored and went for a wander.'

'I was scouting the territory.'

'That's *my* job.'

'No, *your* job is to ask questions. Not to flirt with the target's son.'

'I was not flirting.'

'Sounded like that to me.'

'So this is my fault, is it? You were about to brain my hosts' guard dogs, and it's my fault?'

'I had the situation under control, Darcie. I've dealt with dogs before.'

'It didn't look like that to me.'

'What do you know? You're only a kid.'

Darcie glared at him.

There was a knock at the door.

'Darcie? Darcie? Are you there?' It was Kassim.

'Moment. I'm not decent!' she replied in an unnaturally high voice, shoving Stingo into the shower cubicle. She turned the water on to punish him.

'I was just checking you were OK,' called Kassim. 'There's some trouble outside but nothing for you to worry about. I'll just get changed and wait for you out here.'

'OK.'

Kassim retreated. Stingo emerged from the shower, dripping on to the gold-tiled floor. The deluge seemed to have cooled his temper.

'Towel?' said Darcie, passing him one from a stack by the basin.

'Thanks.' He roughly dried himself, his shoes squelching every time he moved. 'I was looking for your dad. I didn't think they'd let the dogs out with you about,' he admitted.

'I see.' Darcie felt very tired, wishing she could just go home. 'Did you find him?'

'No.'

'Neither did I. I don't think he's here.' She slumped on the bench and put her face in her hands.

Stingo looked down at the top of her bowed head.

'The fire extinguisher was a good idea.'

'Thanks.'

'Braining the dogs wasn't. You were right.' He pulled her to her feet. 'You're doing fine, Darcie. Go back to Prince Charming and find out all you can. I'll get back to the car.'

'And you'll stay there this time?'

'Yes, sir.'

'So, Darcie, you know my son from school, do you?' asked Mr Yaqoubi. He was sitting opposite her at the table, stripping the meat off a skewer with small, efficient bites. Mrs Yaqoubi was watching him nervously as she sipped on a glass of water.

Darcie toyed with her lamb kebab. She could sense the hostility in the question. 'Yes, Mr Yaqoubi.'

'I explained, Abu, Darcie plays football,' Kassim said quietly.

'So I saw.' Mr Yaqoubi said something in rapid Arabic to his son. Darcie didn't need a translation to know that he was complaining about teenage girls throwing themselves all over his lawn.

He turned back to Darcie. 'You talk a lot about my son at home?'

'Not really.'

'Mrs Clutterbuck said you did.'

'Oh, yes. I may have said something . . . about him playing for the school team, I mean.'

'And your parents – what do they do?'

Darcie pretended to be fascinated by the apricots in her couscous. 'My mom's a homemaker. Dad works at the British Consulate.'

'But he's had to go away?'

'Yes.' Why was Mr Yaqoubi so interested in this?

'To a funeral?'

'Yes.'

'But he's coming back?'

She paused, her stomach knotting with fear. 'Yes, I suppose so.'

Kassim was following this exchange helplessly. He looked distressed that his father was giving her such a hard time.

'I heard,' said Mr Yaqoubi in a louder voice, signalling he was reaching his point at long last, 'I heard that your father had been sent home in disgrace – for corruption. Is this true?'

Darcie stared at Mr Yaqoubi. He seemed to be humming with indignation. She didn't know how to answer. He was repeating the version of events Tegla and Winston had been given by the High Commission. Was the story now circulating the whole of the international community? Scandalous gossip spreads like wildfire. Would she have to put up with accusations of family disgrace on top of everything else?

'You'd have to ask my father about that,' she said finally, putting down her knife and fork. *If you know where he is,* was her unspoken thought.

'So you don't deny it?' pressed Mr Yaqoubi.

'I know nothing about it. I haven't seen either of my parents since last week.' Mr Yaqoubi curled his lips scornfully; Darcie felt hot with anger. 'But I do know my father and I don't believe he'd do anything bad.'

'So you've got your mother's friend to invite you to

all the most respectable families in Nairobi, trying to pretend that nothing's wrong – brazening the scandal out? I knew there was something the matter the moment that Texan woman opened her mouth.'

That was it. Darcie stood up. 'Thank you, Mrs Yaqoubi, for a lovely meal. I'm sorry to have put you to all this trouble.' The polite words tripped fluent but meaningless off her tongue. She turned towards Kassim, not meeting his eye. She didn't want to look and find that he despised her too. 'Good luck in the polo tournament.'

'Bye, Darcie,' her classmate said sullenly.

Head held high, Darcie walked out of the room. Her gut instinct was that the Yaqoubis had nothing to do with her dad's disappearance. Kassim's father seemed genuinely outraged that she'd dared show her disgraced face in his house – he wasn't behaving like a man who knew what had really happened. Unless he was a very good actor.

She paused at the front door, considering this possibility. How was she to tell?

Innocent or not, she hated him for destroying her like that in front of the family – in front of Kassim.

Expression fixed in a false social smile, she nodded to the servant and walked swiftly out to the Jag. It wasn't till she reached the seclusion of the back seat that she allowed her face to crumple, giving vent to the tears of humiliation that she had been holding back.

'I want to go home now,' she said, between sobs. She hugged herself, aching for her father's arms around her. 'I want my dad,' she whispered, burying her face in the upholstery, ashamed to be seen crying.

Joel and Stingo looked at each other, but tactfully said nothing as they drove away.

9

Darcie's bedroom at the High Commission was piled high with boxes when she reached home. A note lay on the floor just inside the door.

> We've checked all of them and could find nothing unusual. Can you see if anything is missing? Call us when you get in. G.
>
> PS I don't like your taste in music.

Thoughts of the Yaqoubis pushed from her mind, Darcie threw her schoolbag and sport's kit on the floor. She wasn't sure she could remember every disk she owned, but she had to try. Grabbing the nearest box she started to rummage through, at the same time dialling Aunt Flo on her mobile.

Answering the summons, Gladys and Ben found her deep into her third storage chest.

'Well?' asked Gladys, standing in the doorway.

Ben came into the room and patted her on the shoulder.

'Haven't spotted anything odd or missing,' Darcie replied, 'but I'm not sure I would. But it doesn't make sense anyway: why would Dad hide something among my stuff? Surely it'd be much safer at the villa – or in his office. You've checked there, I suppose?'

'One of the first things we did when he went missing,' said Ben. 'Perhaps he didn't have time to bring it in.'

'Or he may've wanted to keep it to himself for a few days. That was how he worked: building up pieces of the puzzle then coming to us with a full report,' suggested Gladys.

'Well, I don't think it's here,' Darcie declared, shoving the last pile of CDs back into their carton. 'He must've been making up the story about giving it to me to buy himself some time. Do we have any idea who that man last night was working for?'

Ben took a quick look at his boss. She made no sign so he spoke. 'Kenyan government security, Darcie. I'd say he was moonlighting for someone very well placed in the administration. Very risky indeed for him and his boss as coming here violated diplomatic immunity. Someone somewhere is very worried.'

'How does the government fit into all this?'

'Not the government – not officially.' Gladys moved into the room and took a seat at the dressing table. 'Someone in the ranks acting for himself, a minister, a bad apple in a barrel. Remember, I told you that the Ringmaster has all sorts of people dancing to his tune whether or not they know it. Your father must've worked out which minister was involved and managed to get some evidence. I only wish he'd trusted us enough to bring it to us as soon as he got it.'

'Trusted you?'

Gladys gave a sour smile. 'I meant only that I wished he hadn't believed that I would bark at him for an incomplete report. He was probably fussing over loose ends – your dad was very meticulous.'

'Yes, he is.'

An awkward silence fell in the room. Gladys was the first to break it.

'So, what have you to report about the Yaqoubis?

Darcie gave them her impressions as best she could but she was exhausted. Her eyes kept sliding to the clock on her bedside table: it was already eleven and she had not yet got to her homework.

'Good work,' concluded Gladys. 'I agree that Yaqoubi's probably unaware of your father's part in all this, but that doesn't put him in the clear for everything else. The whispers about his links to extremists will not go away. Though his family on the surface seems moderate, we don't really know. After all, we've learned to our cost that the most dangerous terrorists are often the ones who do little to flag up their true intentions. The Ringmaster might still be dealing with him. What next?'

'Nothing till Saturday. Doreen couldn't get me an invitation to Madame Tsui's. In fact, the niece, Pearl, warned me off – told me I wouldn't like it there.'

'Oh? That's interesting.'

'It was kind of sad, really. I don't think she's allowed her own life. She acted more like an employee or something.'

'Well, she probably is. I expect her family has been paid a lot of money to allow their daughter to be groomed for high society. I wonder who Madame Tsui has in mind for her?'

'But she's only my age!'

'You can get married even at your age in many countries, Darcie.'

'It's horrible.'

'That's the way the world works. Get used to it.'

Gladys and Ben said goodnight and left her alone. Darcie yawned. She really felt too tired to do any work, yet it had to be faced. She rummaged in her schoolbag but couldn't find *Great Expectations*. That was odd: she remembered seeing it in there earlier. Tipping the entire contents out on the bed, she picked through the gathered rubbish of the term – notes she'd forgotten to give to her parents, old assignments, empty crisp packets. Then her hand touched a CD in a soft plastic case. It had nothing written on it but Darcie felt her heart pick up its beat. This was what they were looking for – she was sure of it. Her dad must have slipped it into her schoolbag over breakfast knowing she never cleaned out her stuff unless nagged to do so by her mom. It had been safer there than in a Swiss bank vault.

She couldn't wait to see what was on it. Running along to the high commissioner's study, she tapped on the door. There was a light on.

'Come!' called Sir Stephen. He was sitting behind his desk, reading through a pile of official documents. 'Ah, Darcie. Successful day?'

'Yes, sir, very. I think I've found the disk. Do you mind if I look at it?'

'Help yourself. I'll be very interested to see what it contains myself.'

He made way for her at the desk, taking the disk and putting it in the drive. After a few moments of quiet whirring, a file appeared on the screen – 'SecurityZ'. Opening it, she was surprised to be staring at a ground plan of the Country Club.

'What the devil . . . ?' breathed Sir Stephen over her shoulder.

'What is it? What does it mean?'

'It's the security arrangements for this Sunday's polo tournament. From the looks of it, someone in the Kenyan government has leaked them. That's all we need.'

'Can you work out whose copy this is?' Darcie pointed to the information at the top of the screen: 16KA.

'Possibly Kenneth Amollo? He's the minister for trade. But it doesn't make sense. What would he gain from leaking the arrangements?' The high commissioner frowned. 'And what are we going to do about it now we know? I'll have to get Gladys over here at once. Leave this with me, Darcie.'

Darcie lay in bed while lights burned all around the building. The second emergency meeting of the day had been called. She wondered what they were going to do – cancel the tournament? Tell the prince not to come? What would it mean for her dad when it became clear they had found the disk? She hadn't thought of that when she so eagerly rushed to Sir Stephen. Perhaps she should've gone to Gladys first? She would've kept it quiet – now the diplomats were going to crash about all over the sensitive territory that was keeping her father alive.

'I am such a fool,' Darcie told the darkness, feeling too depressed even to cry.

Kassim al Yaqoubi hit the polo ball against the wooden hoarding, making the practice ring resound with a loud crack. He gathered it up and did it again – and again. He was boiling with rage: angry at his father, angry at himself, angry with life in general. Why hadn't he had the guts to tell his father to shut up? He knew why, of course: no one told Abdul al Yaqoubi what to do. But still, Darcie Lock had done nothing. OK, maybe her dad had turned out to be a bad lot, but that was hardly her fault.

'The family shame is shared,' his father had grunted into the awkward silence following Darcie's abrupt entrance. 'You're not to go anywhere near her ever again, Kassim, understand?'

'But Abu –!'

'No buts, Kassim. If I've told you once, I've told you a thousand times about those kind of girls – western girls who don't know how to behave properly. If her father can betray his country after swearing a vow of allegiance, then his daughter can be of little worth.'

It was so unfair, thought Kassim, hanging his mallet next to the one Darcie had used earlier in the evening. The two mallets swayed together for a moment, ticking like clock pendulums in time with each other. He'd been a bit suspicious of her to start with, naturally; that awful Texan woman had been so unsubtle with her attempt to throw the pair of them together. He wondered if Darcie had asked her to do that. If she had, that must mean that she fancied him. Kassim found he didn't mind – he was even smiling at the thought. He'd discovered that evening before his father intervened so disastrously that he enjoyed being with Darcie: she was fun, had a good sense of humour – and she also happened to be very pretty. She didn't seem anything like the portrait of western girls his father always painted: they were all loud, bossy and lacking in morals. Kassim had been at the international school long enough to know that this image was as crude as the caricatures circulating about Muslims all being terrorists. Before dinner, he'd been hoping that maybe she'd want to see him again; now she probably hated him. He wondered how he could face her tomorrow at school, knowing he'd stood by while she was insulted in his own home.

Sometimes he hated his father.

Sometimes he hated himself.

10

08.30, Nairobi: Sunny intervals but with strengthening winds.

'Darcie, you look terrible,' Stingo said cheerfully as she got into the car the next morning.

'Thanks.'

'You really should get to bed earlier you know. Kids of your age should be asleep by nine, ten at the latest,' he carried on, failing to see that she wasn't in the mood for teasing.

She didn't reply but lay back with her eyes closed. Another day at school, another day with no homework done, and another day on which her father might be killed, all thanks to her.

Something landed on her lap with a thump. It was her copy of *Great Expectations*.

'That Miss Haversham woman is a real cow, isn't she?' Stingo said conversationally. 'Using those kids just because she is all twisted up about some bloke who dumped her at the altar. Best thing he ever did if you ask me. And Pip, talk about a kid in need of a good kicking!'

'You read it?' Darcie asked incredulously.

'Well, about a third of it – then I flipped through to the end.'

'My favourite part,' interrupted Joel, 'is the beginning in the graveyard. Very spooky.'

'You've read it too?'

'O level English literature, Cambridge overseas board, class of '73, Miss Lock.'

'I've scribbled down a few things for you so you can write your report on chapter eight,' Stingo said. 'Joel suggested a few things about description and all that arty-farty stuff.'

Darcie opened the book and found the notes, which consisted of remarks like 'Miss Haversham, bad news', 'Estella, very bad news', 'Pip, idiot, deserves what's coming to him'. It may not have been in the style required by Mr Farndon, her English teacher, but

Stingo seemed to have jotted down the essentials on the main characters.

'Thanks. But why?'

'I owe you one. And besides, we thought you've earned a night off from all this. You can't have fun if you're in detention, can you?'

Darcie wasn't sure if she felt like fun just now but she was very grateful. Taking out her English file, she hastily put down some thoughts based on Stingo's notes – enough to wing it, she hoped.

At lunchtime Darcie came across Pearl reading in a far corner of the school grounds. Darcie had come this way to escape Hugo, who seemed to consider her a new leaning post if ever she came within reach. She supposed she should be pleased as it indicated she was on the way to successfully infiltrating his circle, but she found it a strain to maintain her ditsy girl act for extended periods of time and was relieved that she had found someone to talk to who definitely wouldn't consider her shoulder a substitute crutch.

'Hi!' said Darcie, flopping down beside the girl. She shaded her eyes with her Dickens' essay. 'You've almost finished it already?'

Pearl looked up from *Great Expectations* with a distinctly unwelcoming expression. 'I wanted to see what happens to Estella – to see if it turned out all right for her.'

'What? The girl Miss Haversham's grooming to be a man-killer? Don't tell me. I don't want to know. I've not got very far yet.'

'But you spoke well about it in class,' Pearl commented, unbending a little.

'Yeah, well, I had some help on that.'

'Oh?' Pearl seemed interested for the first time in something concerning another person.

'I'm having a bad week. A couple of . . . mates took pity and gave me a hand with the homework. Does your aunt help you with yours or are you just good at everything?'

On the mention of Madame Tsui, Pearl's expression soured. 'No one helps me. I do what I'm expected to do.'

'Perhaps we could help each other then? I don't think my friends will be any use with that maths we've been given.'

Pearl closed her book. Her eyes were sparkling with anger. 'Darcie Lock, stop pretending to be my friend. It won't work.'

'What won't work?' Darcie blushed. She sensed a formidable intelligence in the new girl: Pearl seemed able to see right through her. She had honed in on Darcie's less worthy motives like a shark scenting blood in the water. Yet Pearl had not realised that Darcie really did want to make the newcomer's start at school a little less lonely – her motives had rapidly become mixed with good intentions. But what had happened to Pearl to make her think that even this slight show of friendship had to be rejected? 'Why should I be pretending to be your friend?' Darcie persisted. 'I don't understand.'

Pearl cast Darcie a bitter look as she got to her feet. 'If you don't understand, then perhaps you should read your Dickens more closely.' And she shoved the book inside her bag and walked quickly away.

When the end of school bell rang, Stingo was waiting outside the gates, slouched against a battered Land Rover, dark shades wrapped around his face. Several of the mothers in their four-wheel drives were eyeing him with interest. He certainly made a change from the usual au pair.

'How was school?' he asked drily, opening the door for Darcie.

She got in quickly, aware that the pupils standing around the gates were watching, including Kassim. He hadn't spoken to her during school, but then he never normally did. The difference, Darcie realised, was that today it hurt.

'School was fine,' she said with well practised brevity. 'Where's Joel?'

'I told you. We're having an evening off. He's probably doing his real job driving the high commissioner somewhere.' Stingo started the engine and pulled out on to the main road. 'Sir Stephen just about trusted me enough to be your escort after I told him I also knew a thing or two about evasive manoeuvres.'

'And do you?'

He looked at her in astonishment. 'What do you think the SAS get up to during training – making daisy chains?'

'I've no idea. I'm not the kind of person who pays much attention to all that military stuff.'

'I can see I'm wasted on you, Darcie. You probably don't even know what a warrant officer is, do you?'

She shrugged. 'Nope.'

'It means I earned my rank the hard way, not because I went on some fancy officer's course straight out of college. Hell, Darcie, I spent this afternoon trying to convince Her Majesty's representative to Kenya that my qualifications were up to the job; I hadn't realised I'd have to re-run the whole thing for you.'

'You don't. I'm not dissing you, Stingo.'

He gave a grunt. She knew she'd disappointed him. Soldiering was his world and she'd just displayed her blithe ignorance of all the things that meant anything to him.

'I'm sorry you drew the short straw having to look after me,' she said in an effort to placate him. 'I'll try and be a little more admiring for you, if it'll make you happy.'

He said nothing.

'At least I'm not a boy. You'd've felt much worse if I'd been a boy and still failed to appreciate your no doubt very impressive qualifications for keeping a clueless teenager safe.'

'You're not so clueless.' He'd forgiven her.

'Thanks. So where are we going? I should warn you: I won't be good company. I'm absolutely knackered.' Darcie yawned and lay her head back on the seat.

Stingo glanced at her with a frown. 'That won't do at all. Have a sleep. We're going for a little drive to see some friends of mine. And I should warn you: they won't take to a posh kid who doesn't know to how to have fun.'

Darcie groaned. 'Stingo!'

'Relax. You'll like them.'

Realising she had no say in the matter, she took his advice and fell asleep, only to wake half an hour later as they bumped down an unmade road. They'd left Nairobi and were out in the bush. Grassland stretched before them on all sides, punctuated by the occasional tree. A line of hills hung blue on the horizon. They passed a boy driving a cow along the side of the road, his bare feet floured with dust. This wasn't her idea of a night out. She'd imagined he meant catching a film at the Ya-Ya Centre, not a trek into the wilderness.

'Where're we going?' she asked groggily.

Stingo passed her a canteen of water.

'The lads are staying on an army camp out of the way. The government didn't want us too near civilisation.'

'You're taking me to see your SAS mates?'

Stingo grinned. 'Course. Where else are you going to have a good time in this place? As you'll find out, we make our own fun.'

They passed through a small plantation of trees

and stopped at a checkpoint. Darcie could now see the army base through the wire fence: an airstrip, huts and a concrete building – as a venue for an evening out it didn't look very promising. A Kenyan soldier waved them through after a brief word with Stingo.

'The Kenyans know you're here?' Darcie asked, looking back at the soldier.

'Yeah. They think we're here because of the prince's visit. They don't know about your dad. In any case, we come here often to train. They're used to us.'

Stingo parked the Land Rover in front of the concrete building. Darcie could hear loud music and the sound of laughter from inside.

'This is the mess,' he explained, leading her though the main doors. 'In here and on your right.'

The voices ceased the moment Darcie stepped into a long room occupied by eight men. They all had the same look as Stingo: broad-shouldered, close shaven, scarred, not one unbroken nose among them. Skin tones varied from black to sunburned white. Two held pool cues. The rest were gathered around a card table. All were now looking at her, making no move until Stingo appeared at her shoulder.

'So you did bring her after all,' said a grey-haired man sitting with his feet on the pool table. He got up and handed his cue over to his opponent. 'Good to meet you, Zebra.'

Zebra? Darcie shot a poisonous look at Stingo but he pretended not to notice. It seemed the Yaqoubi twins' nickname for her was going to stick. She allowed the man to shake her hand.

'I'm in charge of this bunch of morons,' the man continued. 'Name's Captain Mahoney, but you can call me Midge.'

'Hi, Midge.' Darcie was beginning to feel less self-conscious as the men turned their attention back to their card game.

'How's Stingo been doing? Keeping you out of trouble?' He led her to the bar and produced a couple of cokes from the fridge.

'Yeah, he's been great. Tied my shoelaces, made

my sandwiches, did my homework, you know the kind of thing.'

Midge grunted. 'Bet he loves it.'

'Every moment, sir,' Stingo replied sardonically. 'As I told you I would.'

'I'll introduce you to the rest of these losers. Gather round, men.' Midge reeled off a list of names. 'Got that?'

Darcie had lost track after the third one. 'Nope.'

'Didn't expect you to. "You there" will do fine for now. Had your coke?'

She nodded.

'Well, you'd better get changed. You can't go on the course in your school uniform.'

'What?' Darcie glanced over at Stingo and saw he had a wicked smile smeared all over his face. 'You'd said we'd come for some fun!'

'This *is* fun, Darcie. I can't sit on my butt all week. Need to stretch my legs from time to time.'

'Fun for you, yes, but not me.'

'Don't tell me you're scared?'

'See, Stingo, I told you the kid wouldn't do it,' said Midge with satisfaction. 'You owe me twenty quid.'

'Give her time, sir. She doesn't know what she's refusing yet.'

'What am I refusing?' asked Darcie.

'A chance of a lifetime – a chance to train with the SAS. Every kid's dream, yeah?'

'Not this one's.'

'You'll enjoy it.'

'Won't.'

'How do you know unless you try?' He paused. 'Oh well, I didn't really expect a girl to get over the first obstacle in any case.'

'Of course I could.'

'Don't believe you.' He took a gulp of coke and turned his back on her.

She thumped him hard in the shoulder blades, angry now that he was ignoring her. 'I can do anything a boy can do.'

This provoked a mocking 'oooh' and laugh from the other men.

'Then show us what you're made of, Darcie Lock.' Stingo flashed his glittering grin at her, knowing he'd won his bet.

As Darcie changed into some cut-down khaki trousers and too big shirt, she cursed her stupid pride for getting her into this. They hadn't had suitable kit in her size so she had to wear her football boots. Her own shorts and short-sleeved shirt had been rejected by Stingo as offering insufficient protection to her arms and legs, resulting in his improvisation of this uniform. She knew she looked ridiculous – like a very baggy scarecrow. At least she had a suitable camouflage jacket thanks to SIS.

'All I need do is get over the first obstacle,' she told herself. 'That would shut Stingo up.'

After a few stretches, she jogged out on to the parade ground where the men were doing a warm-up lap. Each of them was carrying a Bergen rucksack. She fell in beside Stingo.

'How much does that thing weigh?'

'Twenty-five kilograms,' he panted.

'You don't expect me to carry one, do you?'

'Only if one of us carried you and it at the same time. You wouldn't be able to move.'

That was a relief – she didn't fancy even trying to lift one of those packs. 'What's this course then?'

'Child's play,' he replied.

'Why don't I believe you?'

'It's a bush trail – nothing to worry about.'

The squad ran towards what looked to Darcie like a pile of scaffolding. As they got nearer she realised it was a steep ramp: the beginning of the trail.

'Changed your mind?' puffed Stingo.

She said nothing. She was good at sport: I can do this, she told herself.

'Right you lot,' barked Midge. 'This is a timed exercise. You all know your personal bests; your aim is to beat that tonight. Not improving is not an option. You'll do it again until I'm satisfied. As for our guest here,' he winked at Darcie, 'her aim is just to make it round in one piece.'

'And if I drop out?' she called out.

'Stingo buys the first round. He's bet you can do this.'

'And if I make it all the way?'

'You won't.'

'But if I do?'

He shrugged. 'I buy the drinks all night.'

The men cheered.

'Not so fast. My money's safe, lads.'

Stingo sidled over to Darcie. 'Take your time. There's no penalty for improvisation,' he said in a low voice.

'Improvisation?'

'Things that would be cheating for us, but not for you.'

Each man wished her luck before checking their watches. Midge took out a whistle.

'Mark, set, go!'

They were off. Darcie followed behind the pack, having no wish to get involved with the scrum at the front as the men jostled to better their times. The first task was to scale the hill of planks. Her football boots came in useful, giving her good grip. At the top, it was another matter: you had to slide down a rope to the floor. She was the last one to hit the earth but she ran doggedly off on the tail of the stragglers. Midge caught up with her.

'Here to see I don't cheat?' she panted.

'Here to see you don't kill yourself,' he grinned.

Crawling fifty metres under netting was much worse than it sounded. Darcie emerged scratched and sweating out the other end, understanding why Stingo had been so insistent about wearing the right clothes. The men were nowhere in sight.

Midge yawned ostentatiously. 'Had enough?'

She ignored him and ran on. It was getting towards dusk. She didn't fancy completing the course in the dark.

A rope over a muddy pool safely negotiated, Darcie came to her first check: a wall that looked to her at least three metres tall. She ran at it and jumped, but her fingers failed to reach the top. She was just too small. Looking around, she wondered if there was something she could use to help herself over but the course was clear of anything she could lift. Midge checked his watch.

'Well, you lasted longer than I thought,' he said happily. 'Not bad for a kid – and a girl at that.'

Time to put her own training into practice.

'Oh no!' Darcie gasped, clapping a hand to her left eye and gazing helplessly at her feet.

'What's the matter?'

'I think I've dropped my contact lens. It must be just here somewhere.'

'Stay still. I've got a torch.'

Pleased to show off his preparedness in the face of disaster, Midge strode forward and shone a beam at the leaf litter.

'What's that?' Darcie asked suddenly, pointing at the bottom of the wall.

'What?' Midge knelt to take a closer look. No sooner was he on his knees than Darcie scrambled on to his back, jumped up and over the obstacle.

'Sorry. I forgot – I don't wear contacts,' she shouted from the other side. She picked up her pace, not wanting Midge to catch up with her just for the moment as she could hear him cursing her studs for ripping his shirt.

Taking it slowly, she managed the next few obstacles without too much difficulty. The worst moment came when she almost slid off a greasy stepping stone into a bog but, at the last moment, she managed to balance. Midge scowled as he watched from the bank. Darcie bet that he would've liked nothing better than to see her take a mud bath after the trick she'd played on him.

As she approached the end of the course, she met up with the rest of the squad who'd finished and run back to see how she was getting on.

'How much more of this is there to go?' she panted to Stingo. She'd reached the end of her strength and was already thinking longingly of a hot shower.

'Only the death slide.' He pointed to two poles, one tall, one short with a rope stretched between them. 'Up you go. I'm right behind you.'

Darcie's legs had turned to jelly but she could feel him breathing on her heels as he pushed her up. 'I'm not sure about this.'

'Easiest part of the course. It's just your mind telling you otherwise. All you need do is slip your wrists through the loops, run and let go. The rope does the rest. Merlin's on the other side to catch you.'

'Stingo –'

'Come on, you're almost there. I really don't want to buy the drinks if the captain's offered to pay.'

Her body was beginning to shut down. Tired and scared – not a good combination to take to the death slide.

Midge shouted from the ground. 'OK, Stingo, you've proved your point. That's enough.'

Darcie felt a wave of gratitude to Midge, but she hadn't counted on her bodyguard's recklessness now he'd got her this far.

'She's fine, sir. I'll help her up.'

'Darcie, are you OK with this?' The officer's voice sounded very far away. She couldn't muster an answer as she had just reached the wooden platform at the top of the pole. She closed her eyes to stop the world from swaying.

'Up, up and away!' chuckled Stingo.

He seized her by the waist and hefted her on to his shoulders.

'Quick, I can't hold you like this long. Grab the loops. Make sure you get your hands right through and hold on tight.'

Darcie clung on to the padded loops that dangled either side of the wire rope. She'd once been on a ride like this in an adventure playground, but that had only been five metres high over sand; this was twenty metres up over bare earth.

'I can't do this.'

'Yes, you can. You'd better or I'm going to drop you anyway. Are your hands in properly?'

'I'm going to kill you, Stingo.'

'Better hold on then so you can do so later.'

With that he let go and gave her a push over the edge. Darcie screamed as she launched over the void, rocketing towards the platform on the other side. Her scream became a shout. It felt wonderful – like flying. Wind rushed past her; the world had become a streak of colours. All too soon, it was over and she slammed into Stingo's friend, Merlin. He lifted her slightly so she could slip her wrists out of the loops and then helped her down to the platform.

'Can I do that again?' she asked, rubbing the red marks on her arms.

Darcie was the hero of the mess that evening. Midge proved a good sport and bought the drinks with only a few grumbles. He even recounted with approval Darcie's cunning that had enabled her to get over the wall at his expense. She'd never before been the centre of attention in a group of people like this – a group of mates. It was exhilarating.

Dinner had been cleared away and Darcie was dozing happily over her coffee, wondering how long before she'd be able to get to bed, when Stingo tapped her on the shoulder.

'It's time.'

'Time for what?'

'I didn't bring you here just to win a bet, Darcie. We've got the weekend to prepare for.'

His words were like cold water thrown into her face. She shook herself awake. Guilt filled her that the glow of pride at her achievements on the course had briefly dulled the edge of her constant worry for her father.

The soldiers drew their chairs into a semicircle with Darcie in the middle. Riotous during the meal, they were now deadly serious. Midge stood out front and clicked a computer mouse. An image appeared projected on the screen behind him. It was Kassim's home.

'As you all know, Darcie and Stingo returned a zero from the Yaqoubi place yesterday. If Lock is there, then he's very well hidden. Our surveillance has turned up nothing. According to Uncle Sam's satellite imagery, there've been no unexpected movements of people or vehicles. Just a family going about their usual business.' He clicked rapidly through a serious of aerial shots, showing tiny vehicles moving along the drive and around the estate.

'As for Madame Tsui's establishment . . .' Midge now called up a picture of a modest bungalow with a flat white roof. 'Very boring. Just the niece going to and from school. No sign of Madame herself. If she's got Lock, then she's got him somewhere else. Merlin and

B-team checked the Tsui warehouses last night and drew a blank.'

Merlin nodded. 'Just a load of clothes ready for an exhibition. She's got a big trailer, armour-plated by the look of it, to protect her collection. We checked it out, just in case, but it came up clean. It's going to be parked at the Country Club alongside this weekend's polo tournament.'

'Is that still going ahead?' Darcie asked. She'd assumed it would be cancelled after the security breach.

'Yes,' confirmed Midge. 'It was agreed that we can't cancel in case it alarms your dad's kidnappers. Business as usual on that front.'

Darcie was relieved to hear this. The diplomats had been more sensitive than she had feared. 'And the prince?'

'He knows the risks. His view is that rumours of plots and threats follow him everywhere; if he cancelled his holiday every time he heard them, he'd never leave Windsor. Says he's not worried.' An approving murmur ran round the room. 'He's got his own security team, so don't worry about him. Let's worry about you, Darcie. Saturday. Hugo's pad.' Midge flicked to a picture of a farm on the Ngong hills. 'Fortress Kraus. Knife, Jake, Phil and Blister have spent the last few days scouting the place for us and we don't like what we've found. You can't get near the farm without cutting your way through several razor wire fences. The Krauses claim they're to keep in the animals in their private safari park; we say they're to keep the curious out.'

Knife, a dark man with a sharp nose, added, 'My gut instinct says this is our best bet to find the missing man. It doesn't feel right out there – too many guards and wardens crawling over the place for a normal farm – or even a safari park. There were signs of military activity – frequent gunfire and patrols. It could be some crazy militia outfit, guys with desk jobs playing at soldiers at the weekend – that's what the intelligence boys think, but I don't know. Our orders were not to get too close – we didn't want to spook them if they're holding the hostage – but we'd love to turn the place over properly.'

Midge pointed to the image on the screen. 'Yeah, they've got loads of outbuildings – Lock could be kept in any one of them. Trouble is we don't want them to know we suspect anything in case they decide to get rid of . . . any witnesses.' He looked awkward for a moment, before continuing. 'Zebra goes in through the front door Saturday – is that right?'

Darcie nodded. 'Morning. I'm meeting the Krauses at the Stanley. They're giving me a lift.'

Stingo frowned. 'What about me? Do they know I'm coming?'

She hadn't thought of this. 'No. Sorry, Stingo, but I hadn't even met you when the arrangement was made.'

'Well, you're not going without a man on the inside, Darcie,' said Midge firmly. 'We don't know how long it'd take for us to reach you if you get into trouble – that's if you could even get a message out that you needed evacuating. It's by far the most difficult of our locations to penetrate.'

'You'll have to ask Hugo if it's OK to bring your jolly

old uncle along. Ian Lock, your dad's baby brother, come to keep an eye on his niece,' said Stingo, crossing his arms on his chest.

'I'm not sure they'll let me bring a guest.' Darcie wanted someone with her, but the thought of asking Hugo a favour when she hardly knew him was not attractive.

'Come off it, Darcie, all you need do is bat your eyelashes at Hugo and he'll do anything for you.'

'Ugh!'

'You have to or the trip's off.'

'OK, OK. I'll ask him tomorrow.'

'Right,' said Midge, taking over again, 'assuming that Stingo gets inside too, I want him to search the outbuildings while Zebra keeps the Krauses busy. If you find the man, Stingo, get Darcie clear and then we'll bust him out. Zebra, if something goes wrong and Stingo's not around, get yourself somewhere secure, send out an alert on your phone and we'll come for you. We expect you both to check in frequently. If we don't hear from either of you for more than six hours, we'll assume there's a problem and come knocking. That gives you Saturday night, Stingo, to do some serious hunting but I want you to confirm at first light that you're both OK. Any questions?'

'How far away will you be?' asked Darcie.

'We're going to set ourselves up in two teams – one up in the hills as near to the house as we can get, the other close to these outbuildings by the gate on to the Nairobi road. We'll have air backup down the road at Wilson Airport.'

'What should I do if you're coming in to get me?'

'Keep to your room if you can. Stay with your phone. Do nothing to make anyone suspicious. It'll take us a while to bust into a place as heavily guarded as the Kraus estate so it's vital you lay low. Agent Smith has made it very clear to me that your job is to ask questions – but no heroics. If you get a lead to your dad, let Stingo follow it up. Understood?'

'OK.'

'That's it then for tonight. Hopefully, Darcie, you won't see any of us this weekend, but rest assured we won't be far away. You're not on your own.'

At lunchtime on Friday, Darcie walked rapidly around the school perimeter, searching for her target. She'd been too nervous to eat and skipped joining her classmates in the queue for the canteen. The seniors always went first, so there was a good chance Hugo would be outside already. She passed Pearl sitting alone under a cactus-like candelabra tree with its mass of upturned branches, a closed book in her lap. She was staring into the distance, oblivious to everything around her, and her face . . .

Darcie pulled up short. Pearl's face was wet with tears. It was a shock to find that the ice maiden had melted. Darcie knew she had limited time and a job to do, but she couldn't just walk on by. After all, she knew all too well what it felt like to feel lonely and friendless.

Darcie knelt beside Pearl and placed a hand cautiously on her sleeve. 'Are you OK?'

Pearl jumped as if she'd just been stung.

'I'm fine.'

'No, you're not.'

Something snapped inside Madame Tsui's latest protegée. Pearl pushed Darcie off, so that she overbalanced and fell backwards. The Chinese girl was on her feet, striding away.

'Just leave me alone, Darcie Lock,' she shouted over her shoulder. 'It's none of your business – you with your two perfect parents and perfect little rich girl life! What do you know? Nothing!'

Darcie felt her anger rise. That was so unfair! She ran after Pearl and caught her arm, swinging her round to face her.

'Perfect life? That's a very sick joke, but I s'pose you don't know, do you?' Pearl looked confused: she clearly had no idea what Darcie meant. 'You think you're the only one with problems? Fine. Carry on thinking that if you want. But just stop biting the head off anyone who tries to be your friend!'

Darcie turned away and walked off before Pearl had a chance to reply. She knew she shouldn't have lost her cool, but she was so wound up, she couldn't help herself. Making friends with Pearl was as much fun as stepping on a prickly sea urchin.

On the other hand, at least Pearl wasn't all over her like octopus-armed Hugo. Darcie stopped by the doors to the sport's hall. There he was: standing in the centre of a group of his mates by the tennis courts. Well, no time like the present. Still rattled by her encounter with Pearl, Darcie took a deep breath, dredged up a smile from somewhere, and sauntered towards him. A tall, thin Asian boy nudged Hugo as she approached. Hugo swung round and gave her a welcoming smile.

'Hey, Darcie! Were you looking for me?'

She gave a nervous giggle – product of fear rather than pleasurable anticipation as he no doubt thought his due. 'Well, yes, I was.' She flicked her hair over her shoulder as she'd seen other girls do.

Hugo winked at his mates. 'Well then, you've found me.' He took the bag off her shoulder and put it on the ground with his stuff. 'Do you know everyone?'

Darcie shook her head shyly.

'This is Kim.'

A Chinese-American boy nodded in her direction. 'Hi, Darcie. Hugo's told us all about you.'

Darcie wondered uneasily what he had said.

'Helmut, Tony and Johannes,' concluded Hugo, gesturing to the rest of the group. He pulled her closer, leaving his arm resting on her shoulders.

'I hear you're coming out to the estate this weekend,' said Kim, grinning unnecessarily broadly. That seemed to be code for something else as the others all now shared his knowing expression.

'Actually, that's what I wanted to talk to you about, Hugo,' Darcie replied tentatively. She could feel her heart thumping and wondered if he could sense it too as he was so close.

Hugo's grip on her shoulder increased momentarily. 'Not a problem, I hope?' he asked levelly, but his eyes were cold as he looked down at her upturned face.

She gave a small shrug. 'No – well, I hope not. It's just that my uncle's turned up from England and I can't very well leave him on his first weekend in Nairobi.'

Hugo said nothing. Darcie found the silence

painfully awkward. She carried on: 'I was hoping that maybe he could come along too?'

Hugo still did not speak.

'I'm sorry. I shouldn't've asked.' Darcie made to duck out from under his arm, furious with herself for messing this up. She should've found a better time – been more persuasive. Instead, she'd embarrassed herself in front of all his friends. No one in his crowd would have an uncle chaperone in tow – she should've realised that.

'No, it's OK, Darcie.' Hugo gripped her arm to stop her slipping away. He squeezed her closer to his side – too close: she felt trapped by his weight bearing down on her shoulders. 'Bring your uncle. We'd all like to meet him. Just as long as he doesn't –' he stroked her neck with his forefinger, making her shiver '– get in the way.'

Kim and the others sniggered. 'No worries, Hugo, we'll keep him busy for you,' Kim offered.

'That's all right then.' Hugo flashed a smile at Darcie. 'You'd better tell Uncle . . . ?'

'Ian.'

'. . . Uncle Ian to pack his safari gear.'

'OK. Sound's fun.'

'Yeah, it will be.'

The bell rang. Hugo released her, patting her on the rear as she moved away. 'Good girl, see you both at the Stanley then?'

Kassim had to choose that moment to jog by, followed by the other boys from the football team. He'd seen Hugo's gesture – and so had the rest of them. Kassim's eyes widened in surprise. One of the boys gave a wolf whistle.

'Way to go, Hugo!' called one admirer.

Darcie blushed scarlet in the knowledge that all those boys were watching her as she walked off. She wasn't used to being looked at like that – like a girl – particularly by the boys with whom she'd often played football. She hated it.

Darcie's smile vanished as soon as she was out of sight. Hugo had made her feel stupid and cheap; it was little comfort to know she had achieved her goal.

*

'Seems like Hugo's got another girlfriend,' commented the goalie, Bernardo, as he towelled himself off in the changing rooms. 'Makes more conquests than I do saves.'

'Not many then,' muttered Kassim as he stuffed his gear deep into his bag, trying not to show that he was upset by what he'd seen.

'Got to hand it to the man: he works fast,' chuckled Ryan, Kassim's best mate. 'Darcie didn't seem the sort, well, you know – game for a laugh and all that, but not the kind of girl you'd go out with.'

'Yeah, I know. It's like she's changed overnight. I never noticed her legs under her football socks before, but wow!' gloated Bernardo, a dreamy look in his eye.

Kassim stood up abruptly.

'You OK, Kas? You look fed up,' asked Ryan.

'I'm fine.'

'Darcie was round at your place the other night, wasn't she?' Bernardo probed. 'Did you and she –?'

'No, we didn't. She's nice – but she's a friend – *just* a friend.'

Bernardo shrugged. 'Well, if she's *just* a friend, I'd warn her about Hugo. He's a girl-eater from what I hear. Janie told me he's a reputation for turning pretty nasty. Girls go out with him because he's a Kraus – fancy estate and the rest – but it never lasts long.

'Then he boasts about it among his mates afterwards, offers them his second-hand goods, telling them in detail about the girls' good and bad points. Keeps no secrets, the jerk.'

Kassim said nothing.

'Can't help admiring him though,' added Ryan, watching for Kassim's reaction. 'Quick off the mark, taking the prize before the rest of us move a muscle.'

'Darcie Lock is not a prize to be handed about among Kraus's mates,' Kassim said furiously, stalking off.

Kassim waited for Darcie in the corridor as the class filed out from the last lesson. He'd been meditating all afternoon about whether he should say anything and finally decided he had to try. Darcie was in a hurry, bag hastily packed, jacket half on.

'Hey, Darcie, have you got a minute?'

She stopped and looked over his shoulder. Kassim turned to see a big man by a red Jaguar at the gates staring in their direction.

'Your lift home?'

She nodded.

'I won't keep you then. I just wanted to say I'm sorry about Abu. He was really out of order . . . '

'It's OK, Kassim, really. I was embarrassed that I'd been forced on you by my mum's friend.' Darcie seemed really jumpy, eager to get away from him – or from someone else? She kept glancing around as if fearful of seeing a certain person. Hugo perhaps? Was she worried to be seen talking to another boy?

'You weren't forced on us –' Kassim began.

Darcie stopped fidgeting and smiled at him. He felt his insides do a little flip looking into her grey-green eyes. 'Don't lie, Kassim, you're terrible at it.'

'OK, maybe you were – but I'm pleased you were.'

Her face suddenly bloomed with happiness. He realised that she had been looking so strained all week and now for the first time she looked genuinely her old happy self. 'Thanks.'

Seeing her smile made it doubly difficult to say what he had planned.

'Just one thing, Darcie, before you go –'

'Yeah?'

'It's about Hugo. He's got a bit of a reputation with the lads. He's . . . well, you know –'

'Know what?'

'He's not very nice about his old girlfriends,' Kassim said as delicately as he could.

Darcie's eyes widened in surprise. 'I'm not . . . you didn't think that . . .'

'There you are, Darcie!' Hugo swooped down on her from behind and hugged her, lifting her feet from the ground. 'Got you!'

Kassim saw that Darcie looked momentarily panicked before regaining control of herself. She gave a belated squeal.

'Hey, that's enough! Put me down!' she said with a false high laugh.

Hugo dropped her to her feet. 'You're Kassim al Yaqoubi, aren't you?' he said, putting his arm around Darcie possessively.

Kassim nodded curtly.

'My dad knows your old man from the Country Club. You're gonna be playing this weekend, I hear.'

'Yeah, that's right.'

'Well, good luck.'

'Thanks.'

Hugo turned his back, dismissing the younger boy. 'And you, Darcie, I look forward to seeing much more of you tomorrow. Bye for now.' He pushed her towards the waiting Jaguar and sighed as he watched her walk off. 'Cute butt, don't you think, Kassim?'

12

10.00, Nairobi: Hot and humid with risk of heavy and thundery downpours.

Darcie and her 'uncle' arrived together Saturday morning at the Stanley by taxi, luggage in hand, to meet up with the Krauses.

'How do I look?' Stingo whispered, straightening his tie in the foyer mirror.

Darcie didn't think anything could disguise the fact that he never normally wore a suit and had the bearing of a soldier.

'You look fine. So the story is you're a keen rower, best friends with Matthew Pinsent. If anyone asks, you broke your nose playing rugby . . . '

'That bit's true,' he chipped in.

'You're here to do a bit of rock-climbing on Mount Kenya once your babysitting duties are over, which explains the equipment.' She looked down at his large rucksack. 'You normally work as a plumber in west London. Have I remembered everything?'

'Yep. Now my lucky niece: you're a March birthday. Mum called Ginnie, my brother's Michael. They met and married in . . . where was it?'

'Hawaii.'

'Fifteen years ago. One sprog – you. Michael, boring old fart. Me, the interesting black sheep of the family.'

'That's it.' She checked the mirror, pretending to preen her hair. 'Here he is.'

Hugo strode through the lobby, a hungry smile on his face. 'Darcie, you're on time. Fantastic.' He kissed her on the cheek before taking her arm in his. 'This must be your uncle?' He frowned slightly as he studied Stingo.

'That's right. Ian Lock,' the SAS man said, holding out a hand. Hugo shook it, evidently surprised by the firmness of his grip.

'I didn't realise your uncle was so young, Darcie.' Hugo turned back to Stingo. 'There's quite a bunch of us going to be out there this weekend. We're hoping to do a bit of hunting. Do you shoot?'

'A bit,' Stingo shrugged. 'Rowing's more my thing.'

'Sorry, no boats where we're going.'

'Any rocks? I also like rock climbing. Got my sights set on Mount Kenya when Darcie's parents get back.' Stingo tapped his rucksack.

'Might be able to find you something. Not up to the mountain, but maybe a cliff or two. I'll ask the wardens, they'll know.'

'That's great. I'm an outdoors kind of person like my niece here.'

'I can see that.' Hugo tugged Darcie to follow him. 'Come on, let me introduce you to the folks.'

By this he meant his dad, two farmers and their wives from neighbouring estates, and an assortment of their sons and daughters, who were enjoying brunch by the acacia tree. Mr Kraus, a widower, had the heavy-boned looks that he'd passed on to his son, but in his case muscle had turned to fat some years ago. His chair creaked as he got to his feet to welcome Darcie and Stingo.

'Now we're all here, let's get this show on the road,' he said wheezily.

Stingo was given the front seat next to Mr Kraus, leaving Darcie in the back with Hugo. Darcie listened in nervously as Mr Kraus began sounding out Stingo on his background.

'Been to Africa before, Ian?'

'No. South of Spain is about as exotic as it gets for me. Can't stand all that foreign food and funny accents.'

'I know what you mean. You'll be fine with us – home from home, Ian – away from the natives.'

'Great. I've been thinking long and hard about cannibalism ever since I got off the plane. I mean, you never know quite what they're thinking when they look at you, do you?'

Jo Kraus gave a bellow of laughter. 'I wouldn't worry, Ian. They'd probably go for something soft and tender first, like your niece, rather than take you on.'

Darcie grimaced. To fit in with Kraus and his cronies, she supposed Stingo had to pretend he was as deeply racially prejudiced as them, but it was unpleasant to hear. He was too convincing for comfort.

'True, Jo, but she'd only make a mouthful, not worth getting the fire going. Now, your boy: he'd make a better meal.'

'Yeah, he's a fine lad – strong as an ox. And you mustn't worry about Darcie: he'll look after her while we're on the farm, if you know what I mean.'

Stingo laughed rather too heartily. Hugo winked at Darcie.

'So, Jo,' said Stingo, evidently thinking a change of subject was in order, 'have you heard the one about the American, the Chinaman and the African at the UN buffet?'

'No. Go on.'

The SAS man had his host roaring with laughter as he reeled out a series of coarse jokes. As a sign of his approval, Mr Kraus offered him a cigar and both started to puff happily away. Nervous already, Darcie soon felt sick with the smell. She made to wind down the window but Hugo leaned across to stop her, grabbing her wrist.

'Don't. It'll mess up the air conditioning.'

Darcie caught Stingo watching them in the mirror. She didn't like the way Hugo acted as if he had the right to order her every move; she guessed from the glint in Stingo's eyes that he was thinking the same. But it wouldn't be a good idea to start the day with an argument.

'Sorry, I'm not a good traveller,' she said, giving Hugo a wry smile.

'Hey, Dad, you're killing us back here with the smoke,' Hugo shouted, thumping his father on the shoulder.

Wordlessly, Mr Kraus threw his cigar out of the window; Stingo did the same with his. Hugo gave Darcie a smug smile, clearly expecting her eternal gratitude for his gallantry.

'Thanks.' She couldn't bring herself to say any more. It seemed to do, for he stretched out his arms on the back of the seat and began to whistle happily. They were passing through one of Nairobi's shanty towns: makeshift houses slumped at the roadside; children in faded T-shirts and little else watched indifferently as the cars whizzed past, their expressions showing that they knew their two worlds – rich and poor – were never likely to meet.

Darcie tore her eyes away from a football match being played with a punctured ball outside a tin-roofed church. The equipment wasn't up to much, but the boys were good, she noted. And, from the brief glimpse she'd caught, she thought that one of them looked very like her friend, Winston. She wished she could stop to join them. It probably hadn't been him in any case, she told herself, just wishful thinking on her part.

'So, who else is coming this weekend?' she asked, forcing herself to pay attention to Hugo.

'Just a few people from school – Kim, Johannes, Helmut and Pearl. They're not staying.'

'Pearl? I didn't know you and she were friends?'

Hugo flushed with pleasure. 'Hey, and I didn't know you were jealous.' He let his arm drop on to her shoulders – leaning post again. 'Don't worry, she's only coming with her aunt later on. Madame Tsui's showing a few of the highlights of her collection to the ladies – and girls if you're interested – a preview of the stuff she's exhibiting at the Country Club tomorrow.'

'That sounds fun.'

'Yeah? I'm glad you think so. You can see it this evening after dinner. Who knows, you might even be able to persuade your uncle to buy you something.'

'Not likely, mate,' broke in Stingo from the front, showing that he had been listening in all along. 'There's good money in plumbing but not that much.'

'Well, someone's been very kind to Darcie lately. She was wearing a Tsui at the party on Monday, weren't you?' Hugo said. Darcie felt he was probing her for an explanation.

'It was a present – from Mom,' she said hastily.

'You looked drop-dead gorgeous in it. Even so, if my parent was going to spend that much on me, I'd've asked for a car. Hear that, Dad?'

'Well, you wouldn't look very good in a dress, would you?' Darcie shot back.

Mr Kraus laughed. 'Madame Tsui's always on the look-out for new models: you should give it a go, son.'

'I might just do that,' said Hugo, before adding in an undertone, 'I seem to remember that you like men in skirts, Darcie.'

What a creep! It wasn't the smoke making her feel sick now. She sat forward, dislodging his arm.

'Hey, Uncle Ian, have you got any water?'

'Here you go.' Stingo passed her his canteen. 'This should help cool things down a little in the back.'

They had passed through the two razor wire fences ten minutes ago and were now climbing up from the plain to the plateau where the farmhouse had been built to take advantage of the cooler air of the highlands. The views were stunning. Nairobi lay far in the distance, hidden in the grasslands. A cobalt sky arched overhead, leaving Darcie with the impression that they were enclosed in a blue glass globe. They had already seen the first of the animals in the private safari park – a herd of zebra and fleet-footed antelope.

'What else have you got here?' she asked Hugo, excited by the glimpse of a family of wild pig scurrying into the bushes by the road.

'Something of everything – giraffe, lions, even a small herd of elephants. They live way over to the north mostly,' Hugo answered proudly.

'What are they for? Is it part of a conservation project?'

He gave a snort. 'Yeah, right. We're conserving the old ways, Darcie. Can't go hunting now out in the game parks; can only do a bit of controlled culling on our own land. Mind you, it's amazing how many mad lions you get round here, isn't it, Dad? Such a shame they have to be regularly put out of their misery so they're no longer a danger to visitors.'

'I like it!' said Stingo. 'You've actually thought of a way round the game laws – I didn't think that was possible!'

'It's borderline legal, Ian,' explained Mr Kraus. 'But in this country, if you know the right people, keep them sweet, well, you can do just about anything you want.'

'Can't say that about poor old England these days. A man feels so trussed up there – hell, you can't even go fox hunting any more.'

Darcie hoped Stingo was only playing the part of Uncle Ian but he sounded as if he meant what he said.

'You should move out here, Ian. There's a good life to be had for a man like you if you want it.'

'I don't mind admitting I'm tempted. What d'you think, Darcie?'

'And when did you last go hunting, Uncle Ian? I always thought no one could drag you away from the river at the weekend.'

'True, but it's the principle, isn't it, Jo?'

Mr Kraus nodded. 'You're right there, Ian.'

'Anyway, Darcie,' Stingo continued, 'I don't expect you to understand. It's a man's thing, hunting. You're too squeamish – just like your mum.'

They swept up the last few metres of the drive to arrive at the farmhouse. Starting life as an early settler's station, it had been extended many times, reaching a height of luxury that Darcie had never seen in Kenya. Built around a courtyard containing a swimming pool, three sides of the house commanded fine views of the parklands stretched out below. The fourth side, set against the slope of the hill, served as offices and kitchens to keep the family in style. Darcie could see no sign of the normal activity of a farm – no machinery or coffee, tea or sisal plantations. *How did the Krauses make their money?* she wondered.

Hugo fetched her bag as she waited on the veranda. A flash to her left caught her attention – a white man dressed in a warden's uniform was driving along a track winding between some trees. The glitter had come from the sun on his rifle barrel. She then spotted two more patrolling the inner fence, separating the house from the park. Knife had not exaggerated when he'd reported the place to be crawling with security guards.

'I'll show you to your rooms, shall I?' Hugo said, scooping her up with his free arm. 'Why don't you change and come through for a swim? The others will be gathering from now on. We'll have afternoon tea then go out for our hunt at dusk if you want to join us, Ian?'

'Sure. I wouldn't miss it for the world.'

'What about you, Darcie?'

'I think I'll stay here,' she grimaced. 'You hunter-gatherer types go do your thing.'

'No problem. There'll be plenty to amuse you here.'

Hugo showed her into a bright white room with double doors leading out on to the poolside.

'I've put you in here, Darcie. My room's next door. Ian's is across the hall. I'll leave you to it, shall I?'

'Thanks.'

He hefted the bag on to the bed.

'What have you got in here, Darcie? It weighs a ton.'

'Just my make-up bag and a few clothes.'

'Women!' Hugo tutted to Stingo. 'They're all the same.'

Darcie wondered how many other girlfriends Hugo had brought home. Quite a few, she guessed, from the practised air he had. But if he thought this weekend was the beginning of a new romance, then he had another thing coming to him. She was already counting the hours until she could escape back to Nairobi, hopefully having found her dad.

She changed into her swimming costume and was about to walk out to the pool when there was a soft tap on the door.

'Come in.'

Stingo slid in wearing shorts and a T-shirt. He put his finger to his lips, took her into the bathroom and turned on the taps so that the water thundered into the tub.

'Just in case the rooms are bugged,' he explained.

'You can't go out like that! Look at your tattoos!' Darcie exclaimed, grabbing his wrist and shoving the military style logo under his nose.

He shrugged. 'Loads of guys have them. I did three years in the RAF before being chucked out, OK? That'll do. But that's not what I wanted to talk about. Did you notice the guards?'

Darcie nodded.

'Mercenaries if ever I saw one. I probably even know some of them.'

'What if they recognise you?'

He shrugged. 'Too late now, but I'll try and make sure our paths don't cross.'

This wasn't very reassuring. 'And what are mercenaries doing patrolling a safari park?'

'Good question. I think we've both realised this is no farm we're on. It has the feel of an army base if anything.'

'My dad thought Kraus and his cronies were trying to overthrow the government.'

'If that's so, then they've got plenty of men about the place to take advantage of any crisis.'

'But they can't seriously expect Kenyans to want a bunch of white farmers to take over power?'

'No. But they might have a stooge who they think they can control – a puppet in the wings.'

'What, like that minister for trade, Kenneth Amollo?'

Stingo nodded. 'From what your people at the villa told me, Kenyans are already disenchanted with the new regime. If there's a crisis and the president does badly, someone like Amollo might be able to push himself to the top. There are probably already outside business interests investing in the new people.'

'Investing?'

'Well, it won't be settled over tea and sandwiches on the lawn of the presidential palace, will it? They need money for weapons, mercenaries and for buying off corruptible sections of the army. If they're very lucky, the whole thing might drop into their lap with hardly a shot being fired.'

'What kind of crisis would do that?'

'I dunno. That's what the intelligence people have got to find out.'

'Do you think the tournament tomorrow has anything to do with it?'

'I can't see how at the moment. The Country Club's hardly the obvious place to start a coup. The president's not even going to be there.'

'What shall we do?'

'I'll report in and then go and scout out the outbuildings back down the road. If our hunch is right, they should have enough weaponry here to mount a serious challenge to loyal government forces.' He slipped his hand to the waistband of his shorts, checking something tucked under his shirt at the back.

'What's that?'

'A Browning 9mm.'

'You've a gun?'

Stingo raised his eyebrows.

'Sorry, of course you do. I just . . . I just hate guns.'

'I'm not surprised since your only experience of them was to have one shoved in your neck. There are too many guns and even more people who don't know how to control them. Don't worry, Darcie, it's just a precaution.'

'And me? What should I do while you're looking around?'

'You go for a swim. Look pretty. Be charming. We don't want them to think anything is wrong.'

'Be careful won't you?'

'This is my meat and drink, Darcie. I won't be seen. I won't be caught. If they ask, tell them I've gone looking for rocks to climb.'

Darcie was pleased to find that she was expected to do very little that afternoon except lay in the sun and swim when she felt like it. Hugo seemed to think it enough that he could present her to his guests like a painting he'd recently bought, a brief chance for her to be admired, then he moved on, acting as host while his father stayed closeted with his cronies in his study. She had plenty of time to read her novel, progressing far enough to understand how Pearl might see herself in Estella, the girl being groomed to torment her male admirers. No wonder she had been wishing for a happy ending for that character. Pearl had been looking for some hope for herself.

'How're you doing, Darcie?' Hugo perched on the seat beside her and handed her a drink.

'Fine. Enjoying the rest. I've had a busy week.'

Hugo brushed her hair off her shoulder and touched

the scar left by her assailant. 'How did you do that? I noticed it earlier.'

'Oh that?' Darcie forced herself to smile. 'Didn't I tell you? I got shot at by a mugger.' She watched him closely to see how he would react. Did he know already?

'You're joking?' He did seem genuinely surprised.

'It's nothing. Bullet just grazed me. I got away.'

'Poor Darcie. I'm sorry: we should take better care of you, shouldn't we?'

What did that mean exactly? 'It's nothing,' she repeated.

He put his arm around her. 'Well, you stay here out of harm's way while we go out for our expedition. Where's that uncle of yours got to?'

'Went looking for a climb, I think. He can't sit still for two minutes. He's famous in the family for it.'

'Oh.' Hugo no longer looked happy. 'He should've asked someone to go with him. It's not safe out there on your own.'

'Worrying about me, are you?' Stingo threw a towel on the seat beside Darcie. 'I'm back. Found a nice place to scramble just behind the house. Ready for a swim, Darcie? Race you to the end?'

Darcie threw her book aside. 'You bet.'

They both ran to the edge of the pool and dived in, showering some of the guests lounging on the side with spray. Darcie let the water stream over her like silk, then broke into a smooth crawl, reaching the end first. Stingo bobbed up beside her a moment later.

'Blimey, niece, I didn't know you could swim like a fish,' he said, splashing her.

Darcie looked over her shoulder. Hugo was still watching them, his expression hard to read. 'Keep splashing. Tell me what you found.'

'What we thought. Bloody arsenal down there.'

'Dad?'

'No sign.'

She dived into the water and pulled his legs from beneath him. Under the cover of her screams and shrieks as he retaliated for the ducking, he said, 'I don't like it, Darcie. I don't even like the way that creep is treating you – it's not healthy. I think we should pull you out – send you home with stomach cramps or something.'

Darcie went underwater again, pulling him down with her. She shook her head vigorously, hair floating around her like a mermaid's. No way, she mouthed in bubbles. Striking out for the other end of the pool, she swam away from him and got out. Hugo was waiting at the edge. He handed her a towel.

'Everything OK? Looked like he was trying to drown you.'

Stingo climbed out and shook himself like a dog just out of a bath, showering Hugo with water.

'I'm fine. Uncle Ian's always been a bit rough.' Darcie gave Stingo a shove. 'I'm used to it.'

'It's me you should be worried about, Hugo. My niece is merciless in the water,' smiled Stingo, pushing her back.

'You'd better get ready if you're coming with us, Ian,' Hugo said coldly, interrupting the family playtime.

'I think I'll get changed too,' added Darcie. 'Gets a bit chilly up in the hills, doesn't it? See you at dinner.'

Stingo followed her out of the courtyard, taking a shortcut through her room. Once out of Hugo's sight, he pulled her into the bathroom.

'Haven't you got your own shower?' she said, hoping to avoid another conversation with him. 'You know we really should stop meeting like this,' she quipped as he turned the bathwater on again.

'Shut up, Darcie, and listen. I'm reporting in and will tell that Smith woman that she should order you out. You've done your bit by getting me in here. I can't do my job properly while I'm worrying all the time about a fourteen-year-old stuck in the middle of a place packed full of mercenaries, being romanced by the biggest creep I've ever laid eyes on. No offence, Darcie, but his interest in you doesn't seem right. He's up to something – and I'm not talking boy-meets-girl stuff. We know that Amollo wanted to use you against your dad; what if the Krauses brought you here for the same reason? I know we've no proof, but what if they're all in this together?'

Darcie hung her head. He was right, of course.

She didn't want to become a liability.

'I have to admit that what I saw this afternoon scared the living daylights out of me,' said Stingo. 'We'd always thought that these guys were just playing at soldiers – a bunch of harmless loonies firing a few rounds off at the weekend. But it's much worse. They've got every kind of small arm and light weapon you could care to name – and some heavy stuff. They've even got armoured cars down there – old Soviet cast-offs but they'll do the job all right. This is no place for a kid.'

She'd heard enough. 'All right. Tell them to send a car for me after dinner. I can head back with the other Nairobi guests after the fashion show. I'll say to Hugo I'm not feeling well – that won't look odd.'

'Good. And Darcie?'

'Yeah?'

'As your uncle, I think I should advise you to keep Hugo Kraus at arm's length.'

'Don't worry, I'm trying to. Anyway, I've come prepared.' She picked up her special bottle of mosquito repellent from the shelf over the basin and slipped it into her handbag. 'That should get rid of the most persistent bugs.'

Up in the hills, overlooking the Kraus estate, Captain Midge Mahoney radioed into headquarters in the grounds of the High Commission.

'Report at 1600 hours from Stingo and Zebra, ma'am,' he said. 'Kraus place is full of weapons – it seems they've found one end of our smuggling operation. Stingo requests we send car for Zebra at 2200 hours so she can leave with the other guests. He thinks it's too dangerous for her to stay tonight. Situation volatile.'

'What do you think, Captain?' asked Gladys Smith calmly. 'Is he panicking?'

'Stingo has a cool head, ma'am. He doesn't panic.'

'And what of the girl?'

'I can see her quite clearly from here.' Midge trained his binoculars on the courtyard from his vantage point of a bluff overlooking the house a mile away. 'She spent the afternoon by the pool and has just returned there. She's talking to another girl – Pearl Cheng, I think, but I can't be sure from this distance.'

'Does she look in any immediate danger?'

'No, ma'am, or I wouldn't be talking to you about it, would I?'

'Point taken.'

Gladys looked up at Ben who was listening in on the conversation on the other side of the table. Agent Eagle had joined them and was chewing on a toothpick nervously.

'What does your surveillance team tell us?' she asked the American.

'Madame Tsui had two container loads heading towards the farm. Rather excessive for a fashion show, wouldn't you say? I'd very much like to see what's in them. It could give us the proof we need that she's the one behind the smuggling operation.'

'And Darcie?'

'It's your call. If you pull her out tonight, it might just make them more suspicious, preventing your man on the inside getting anywhere near those containers.'

'But, ma'am, she's only fourteen.' Ben risked speaking out of turn as he knew he wouldn't get another chance. 'We can't play fast and loose with her life.'

'Don't you think I know that, Ben?' snapped Gladys. 'She's my responsibility. Let's look at the facts. She appears under no immediate threat. My reading of the situation is that Warrant Officer Galt is just getting jittery because she's an unwelcome distraction. If we leave her there tonight, we give him twelve more hours to look at those containers, find Michael and clinch this for us. If we take her out, we lose this chance and possibly lose Michael too.'

Agent Smith turned to a small video screen on the table beside her.

'Did you follow all this, sir?'

Back in London, the Director of Regional Affairs shifted at his desk. His face was in shadow.

'Of course,' he said.

'Your orders?'

'If there's the slightest chance we can bring Michael out alive without undue risk to the . . . er . . . intelligence operative, then we should.'

'But, sir,' said Ben, 'if we have to send in the SAS to get her out, there'll inevitably be a delay as they bring up the helicopter. She might have to fend for herself for a couple of hours if things turn sour. She's got next to no training – she's only fourteen for heaven's sake –'

'Thank you, Agent Bulldog, I quite understand the situation,' cut in the man on the video screen. 'We also know she's resourceful and quick-witted: we can trust her to keep her head. Besides, I can't imagine that the Krauses have anything to gain from harming her – we would not have sent her in if we thought that. No, she must stay.'

'I agree.' Gladys leant back to the radio. 'Captain Mahoney, request for car denied. Zebra to stay at her post until further notice.'

The hunting party disappeared in the three Land Rovers, leaving the house to the ladies. Darcie decided it was time to do a bit of scouting of her own before the car came to fetch her. The first person she bumped into by the pool was Pearl.

'Hi.' She made to walk on. She'd had too many rebuffs from Pearl to expect to be welcome.

'Darcie, can I have a word?' Pearl shot an anxious look towards her aunt who was speaking to Mr Kraus by the bar in the far corner.

'Of course.' Pleasantly surprised that Pearl wanted to talk to her at long last, Darcie sat down and pretended to soak in the sun. Pearl copied her example.

'You've got to get out,' whispered Pearl. 'I don't know what's going on but I heard my aunt discussing you on the phone as we drove here.'

'Discussing me?' Darcie tried not to show it but she felt as if Pearl had just dropped an ice cube down her back.

'Yes. She said she had something planned for you. Believe me, when she says that it never means anything nice.'

They lay side by side for a few moments as Darcie

digested the news. She could hear the tap-tap of high heels heading towards them.

'Don't worry. I'm out of here soon,' she murmured as she made a great show of flicking through a magazine some other sunbather had discarded.

'Darcie Lock isn't it?'

She put the copy of *Vogue* aside and looked up into Madame Tsui's stony eyes. She wore a glittering jet necklace round her neck and two black pearl earrings.

'I am very pleased to meet you. My niece has told me that you have been very friendly towards her this week.'

Darcie flicked a glance towards the girl beside her, but her classmate was as expressionless as normal. 'I tried to make her feel welcome.'

'Indeed you did. I wondered if you would care to help me tonight?'

'How?' gulped Darcie.

'I need another model for my clothes. I saw you in one of mine earlier this week, didn't I? I thought you looked very good. You would be doing me a great favour if you accompanied Pearl on the catwalk.'

Darcie almost laughed. Was this what Pearl had overheard being planned in the car – an invitation to act as a clothes horse?

'I'm happy to help but I've no idea how to walk and do all that model stuff.'

'Are you busy now?'

Darcie held up her empty hands. 'Not really.'

'Then I'll teach you how it's done.'

Darcie had to keep telling herself that the woman in front of her was a drug runner and a seriously unpleasant person because Madame Tsui reminded her strongly of her old ballet teacher in Berlin some years ago. She remembered the tutor's precise teaching style with affection, despite the fact that they had both rapidly come to the agreement that the six-year-old Darcie was never going to make it as a dancer. Still today Darcie knew she was not able to crack the mystery of elegance and poise into which other girls were initiated without problems.

'One, two, three and turn. Hand on waist. Swing your hips. Hold it. Back two, three and off.'

Madame Tsui clapped the rhythm out remorselessly, making Pearl and Darcie pace up and down the improvised catwalk in the dining room. She'd given them both high heels to wear, but said the costumes had not yet arrived.

'They are from my newest collection. You will wear casual, cocktail dress then evening gown. Just six between you, but that is enough.'

To be honest, Darcie found mincing up and down the room in high heels more difficult than the obstacle course she'd managed earlier in the week.

'This is not my natural element. Give me football boots any day,' she whispered to Pearl as they crossed in the middle, raising a rare smile from the other girl.

After an hour of this, Madame Tsui called a halt. 'You can leave, Pearl. Go and talk to Mr Kraus. He's expecting you.' Pearl bowed and left the room. 'And Darcie, that was good. You've learned very fast. You have an energy that makes up for a certain awkwardness in your movements.'

'Thank you.' Darcie tried to guess what Madame Tsui was thinking as she stood there in her close-fitting black dress, her expression as mysterious as the black pearls suspended from her ears. Both had a surface beauty that concealed the grit within. Her face was ageless – so smooth she could have been anything from thirty to sixty.

'Have you ever thought of modelling?'

Darcie wouldn't in a million years have guessed that this was what had been on the woman's mind. 'No, never.'

'You have the right figure – you're tall for your age, striking rather than beautiful. Perhaps you should consider it.'

'I will.' She had – for two seconds – and decided it was the last thing she wanted to do with her life.

'I'll see you back here at eight then. You won't let me down will you? I'm counting on you.'

'Of course not.'

Darcie felt she had been dismissed. She hobbled

outside, slipped out of her shoes with a sigh of relief, and padded barefoot back to her bedroom. That had been an odd way to spend the early evening and the worst of it was that she'd had no chance to look around the house. Part of her wondered if that had been Madame Tsui's aim in keeping her rehearsing. Now, she'd have to pack so that she was ready to go when the car arrived and then there would only be time for a quick bite at the buffet before the fashion show.

Before tackling the clothes she'd strewn around her room, she knocked on Stingo's door.

'Uncle Ian?'

No reply. She could hear Hugo whistling in his room next door to hers so she knew the hunting party must have returned. She tapped hesitantly. Hugo threw the door open.

'Hey, Darcie, have fun while we were out?'

She wrinkled her nose. 'I'm not sure. Madame Tsui's roped me into her fashion show.'

'Great. Might be worth watching then.'

'How was your outing?'

'Not bad. Quite entertaining really.'

'Do you know where Uncle Ian is?'

Hugo shrugged. 'Search me. You know, he turned out to be a crack shot. There's more to that uncle of yours than meets the eye, isn't there?'

She could feel his gaze as if she were sitting under a sunlamp. 'Is there? He's just Uncle Ian to me. Well, if you do see him, can you tell him I was looking for him?'

Next she checked the pool in case Stingo had gone for a late swim, but there was no one there except the servants laying out the buffet. Back in her room, she paced fretfully to and fro, wondering just how worried she should be. Perhaps he'd merely gone scouting again and she'd be doing him no favours to draw attention to his absence? With a sigh, she got out her phone and rang Aunt Flo.

'Hi, it's me.'

'Everything all right, Darcie?' asked Gladys.

'Yes and no. Can't find Uncle Ian – but that might not mean anything.'

'Careful what you say, Darcie. Remember the room might be bugged. Make sure your answers give nothing away. All right. Are you listening?'

'Yes, Aunt Flo.'

'We think he may have gone looking at the new containers Madame Tsui brought with her this afternoon. We need the evidence to connect her to the weapons out there.'

'OK. What time's the car coming?'

'I've cancelled the car.'

'What?' Darcie felt horribly shaken by this news. She'd been comforting herself with the idea that she'd soon be out of there. 'But I thought –'

'You're making excellent progress. We don't want to do anything to upset them, do we?'

'No, I s'pose not.'

'Sit tight. Press the panic button if you need to, otherwise try and see this through to tomorrow morning. Captain Mahoney's team are watching you the whole time.'

'I'm not sure. What if Uncle doesn't come back?'

'Do you really need a babysitter, Darcie?' asked Gladys sharply. 'I thought you had more guts than that. What about your dad, or have you forgotten him?' Ben shook his head, deeply disapproving of this blackmail on the part of his boss. Agent Eagle spat out a peanut shell, trying to look as if this was none of his affair.

Darcie sat down on the bed, tears brimming in her eyes. 'Of course I haven't forgotten,' she said thickly.

'So do you want to press the panic button? Do you want Captain Mahoney and his men to pull you out?'

'No.'

'Good. I'll see you tomorrow, Darcie.'

'OK.'

Gladys put down the phone and met the accusing eyes of her two companions.

'What?' she asked irritably.

'The kid wanted out,' said Ben huskily.

'Every agent hits a wall at some point in a mission. It's my job to stiffen their backbone for them. I warned her I'd do so when I took her on.'

'Yes, but –'

'No buts, Ben.' Gladys opened radio contact with Captain Mahoney. 'Zebra checked in.'

'Everything OK?'

'Yes. She's doing fine.'

Darcie had no appetite for the buffet that evening. The poolside looked enchanting: candles burned on all the tables and ledges, providing a flickering magic. A cool breeze fluttered the hems of the ladies' chiffon and silk dresses, and rippled the floodlit water of the swimming pool. Gentle classical music poured from the sound system, giving a sophisticated undercurrent to the chitchat of the guests. Darcie moved around, holding a glass of sparkling water, never coming to rest for too long in case she had to talk to someone. Gladys had told her not to worry, to play her part and keep calm, but her mind was flitting butterfly-like from one fear to another. Where was her dad? What had happened to Stingo? Did Madame Tsui have anything else planned for her? Pearl had seemed really worried. Darcie was almost relieved when it was time for the fashion show so at least she could have some distraction.

'Have you done this before?' she whispered to Pearl as they put on their first outfit. Two Chinese assistants stood at hand to offer silent help with zips and fastenings.

Pearl nodded. 'Yes, in Singapore. Auntie used to give private shows to her business contacts. The worst part is the quick changes. As there's only two of us, Auntie will have to say something in between each set.'

'I feel a bit sick.'

'So do I. It's just nerves.'

Darcie was surprised that Pearl could feel anything as normal as stage fright.

'You needn't worry. You look great, Pearl.'

The girl frowned. 'I wish I didn't. Everything would've been very different if I just looked like my sisters.'

'Oh?' Darcie didn't risk showing too much interest, knowing it would only put Pearl off. She pretended to be far more interested in the leather straps of her shoes.

'Yes, I'd still be at home. Probably promised to some stupid farmer.' Pearl gave a brittle laugh. 'Listen to me! I've travelled half-way round the world and still ended up earmarked for a farmer – a fat, dumb power-crazed bigot.' She stopped and put her hand over her mouth, tears filling her eyes. 'Sorry, I didn't say that. Don't you dare tell anyone I said that.'

Darcie shook her head. 'I promise. As far as I'm concerned, you didn't say anything.'

She watched as Pearl headed for the door to make her entrance. Poor Pearl. It did not take a genius to work out which stupid, fat farmer had negotiated with Madame Tsui for a young wife. Did Hugo know his father had plans to give him a stepmother of his own age? It was disgusting. She had to do something to help. Perhaps the high commissioner could save Pearl from this – take it up with the Kenyan authorities at least?

If you want to help Pearl, you have to get out of here first, she told herself soberly.

Pearl walked into the spotlights, all traces of her

distress hidden by a Mona Lisa smile.

And if you want to do that, you've got to play your part. Be charming, act natural, relax, Darcie told herself.

The first and second journeys down the catwalk passed without her doing anything too embarrassing. She didn't fall on her face or collide with Pearl. The last was the one she most feared as she guessed the evening dress would be long and the shoes ridiculous. She was right on both counts. Her dresser slid a tight-fitting silk gown with a long train over her head and pulled it firmly down to the ground.

'How am I supposed to walk in this?' Darcie whispered frantically. She felt as if she had just been squeezed into a light-weight sleeping bag. 'Bunny hops?'

'Small steps,' advised Pearl as she emerged from a matching dress, white to Darcie's blue.

Darcie swore when she saw the shoes – instruments of torture sewn with sequins.

With practised ease Pearl sashayed off to the applause of the audience. Darcie prepared herself for major humiliation. The only consolation was that at least Kassim was not here to see her prancing about in this stuff. She took a deep breath, counted to ten, then followed.

'Hand embroidered in Java, these gowns have been made from silk from my own silk farms in Thailand.'

Madame Tsui's words floated over Darcie's head like dandelion seeds. She felt light-headed, seeing things in flashes. Hugo staring at her, wolf-whistling, his teeth glinting white in the spotlights; Mr Kraus watching Pearl, his prospective bride, gliding before him in her white dress; Kenneth Amollo, the minister for trade, and his wife sitting in the front row. A bodyguard behind them with a thick gold bracelet.

Darcie stumbled as she reached the crossing point with Pearl. The other girl reached out and caught her arm to steady her.

'I feel strange,' Darcie whispered.

'Keep smiling – we'll walk back together.'

Pearl supported her back to the changing room. Out of the public eye, Darcie sat down and put her head between her knees.

'I think I'm going to faint.'

'When did you last eat?' asked Pearl practically.

'Can't remember.'

'You should always eat before a show.' She poured Darcie a glass of water and handed her a banana from the display of fruit on the sideboard. 'Don't get up before you've kept that down.'

The sound of clapping outside told them that Madame Tsui was taking her bow.

'We should really go and join her,' Pearl frowned.

'You go. I'm going to my room before anyone catches me here.' She meant Hugo. She couldn't stand the idea of being near him now. Besides she had to tell Gladys about Amollo.

Pearl nodded and returned to the stage. Discarding the banana skin and empty glass, cursing herself for being so dim as to forget to keep up her energy levels, Darcie took the passageways inside the house heading back to her bedroom. She had some glucose tablets in her bag. She'd chew a couple of those, phone Gladys, change, then check to see if Stingo was back.

Hearing voices ahead, she ducked behind the nearest door to avoid getting caught in conversation. Footsteps approached. She saw through the crack in the door that it was Hugo's dad leading another man along the corridor, heading her way.

'We'll leave the ladies to the serious business of shopping, shall we?' Mr Kraus said gruffly. He marched straight into the room in which Darcie had taken refuge. 'I have a very fine whiskey you might appreciate.'

'I hope my wife remembers how much the government pays me,' said Kenneth Amollo, slumping into a chair. 'I cannot afford even a pair of the shoes on show tonight.'

Darcie held her breath and surreptitiously pulled the long train of her dress out of sight. They were in the room with her now: she couldn't leave without being seen. She had to pray they wouldn't close the door.

'You soon will. You'll be able to buy her the whole collection if you like.'

She could hear the chink of glasses as Mr Kraus poured the drinks.

'Do not tell me the details, Jo, but are you sure everything will go to plan tomorrow?'

'The arrangements for the tournament are well in hand. Our man on security will plant the device in the young Yaqoubi's tack just before he saddles up. When it goes off, people will immediately assume that it's the work of fundamentalists – a suicide bomber.'

Darcie went cold. She closed her eyes, forcing herself to listen.

'There are enough rumours about the family already to make that a natural assumption,' continued Mr Kraus. 'We'll issue a statement from an as-yet-unknown group claiming responsibility.'

'And . . . er . . . fatalities?'

'Hard to predict as the timer is set to go off in the middle of play. The boy of course. Anyone in a radius of ten feet or so. There'll certainly be injuries. You can't do this without shedding blood, you know.'

'I know that.'

'We'll have our men ready to add to the mayhem. In the confusion that follows the attack on the royal visitor – you know the kind of thing we expect: outrage from the West, calls for a crackdown on extremists – the president will be shown to be incompetent. We'll release the bits of compromising evidence we have about him, pump up the calls for a strong man to take charge, and then it's your moment. Our men behind you, you take power, promise new elections and then, Mr President, Kenya is yours.'

'You make it sound very easy, Jo.'

'It is as long as you keep your nerve.'

'But what about the disk? It's been haunting me since I handed it over to that man. I was a fool to think he was on our side. What if they know?'

'Don't worry. We've thought of something to clear that small obstacle out of the way.'

'What?'

'I thought you didn't want to know the . . . shall we say . . . less savoury details?'

'I don't.'

'Then trust us. We've come too far to let this fail now. But, Ken, I should warn you: you've made one mistake – Madame Tsui won't forgive you if you make another. She wants to see a good return on her investment.'

Three loud explosions sounded outside. Darcie jumped. Had the SAS come to pull her out?

'What's that?' asked Kenneth Amollo, the ice cubes rattling in his glass.

'Don't worry, old man. It's just the fireworks. Let's go and enjoy the display – a foretaste of what's to come.'

The men left. Darcie waited a few moments until the coast was clear and then ran for her bedroom. They'd set up Kassim! It was too horrible to think about. She had to report this at once.

She burst into her bedroom and fumbled blindly around on the bed for her phone. A flash from a rocket outside suddenly lit up the room, revealing someone standing in the French windows watching her. She gave a scream.

'Did I startle you? Sorry, Darcie. I just wondered where you'd got to.' Hugo stepped forward. 'Are you OK?'

'Yes.' Even she could hear that her voice sounded strangled.

'Good.' Hugo smiled and stretched his arm out towards her. 'Then I thought you might like to come for a little walk in the moonlight with me.'

'I . . . er . . . ' She gripped the phone tightly, desperate to make her call.

He moved towards her and eased the phone out of her hand.

'The kind of walk I have in mind doesn't go well with this.' He chucked it on to the bed. While his back was turned, Darcie picked up her hairband, flicking the small microphone on.

'Transmission from Zebra,' said Merlin, hunkered down beside Midge, headphones clamped to his ear.

'What's going on?'

Merlin shook his head. 'Not sure.'

Hugo moved closer and slid his arm around her. 'You look amazing in that dress, Darcie, has anyone told you that?'

'No.'

'You're trembling.'

'A little.'

'There's no need to be nervous. Hasn't anyone taken you for a walk in the moonlight before?'

Merlin grinned at Midge. 'I don't think Zebra meant us to hear this. Sounds as if she might be getting her first kiss any moment now.'

Darcie pushed the band on to her hair, hoping she'd get a chance to alert the team by saying something more specific. 'OK, I'll take a walk. I wanted to see the fireworks.'

Hugo brushed his fingers through her hair and pulled off the hairband. 'I like your hair loose.'

'I like it tied back.'

He dangled the hairband from his fingers. 'Humour me, Darcie, just this once.' His expression was mocking. It was almost as if he knew.

Darcie was both scared and angry now. She grabbed her clutch bag from the table by the door. 'You've no objection if I take this, I hope?' she asked with a touch of sarcasm.

'As long as it won't interrupt us. What's in it?'

'Mosquito spray.'

'Very wise. Malaria can be a killer. Give it here, I'll put it in my pocket and you can ask me for it when you need it.'

She handed it over without a word.

'Ready?' he opened the door for her.

'Yes.'

Up on the bluff, Midge was getting restless.

'How's Zebra doing?'

Merlin grinned and flicked the receiver so Midge could hear the static fizz. 'It's gone very quiet.

I'm glad I'm not her mother or I'd be really worried now.'

'Save the jokes,' said Midge, training his binoculars on the house as the fireworks flashed above them. Everything seemed fine, but his gut was telling him different. 'Has Stingo checked in?'

'Nope. Still a few hours until he's officially beyond his deadline.'

Midge rubbed his forehead to clear the sweat from his brow. This was the hardest part of any mission – the wait. He would've liked to go in and get the girl now but his orders were to stand by until she requested assistance. Like as not, he'd just interrupt her necking with that blonde boy in a corner somewhere and blow the mission. They had to sit tight.

'Keep listening. Let me know if anything changes.'

Hugo towed Darcie with him through the crowds by the poolside. The firework show was reaching its conclusion with starbursts over the hills. A line of cars was waiting on the drive to take the guests back to

Nairobi, a couple of hours' drive away.

'Let's go somewhere quieter,' he breathed in her ear.

'I'd like to stay here.'

'No, I've got something I want to show you.'

'Can't it wait?' She felt pathetic: she should just knee him in the groin and run. But where to? She was surrounded by his friends. Her gaze met Pearl's and she tried to signal her to come to the rescue but Madame Tsui was directing her niece into a car.

Hugo brushed her hair off her shoulder. 'No, it can't wait, Darcie. In fact, I'm certain you're eager to see this too.'

'See what?'

Hugo steered her into the kitchen wing and opened a door that lead into the hillside itself. 'Our cellar. The finest store of wine this side of the Mediterranean.'

'I'm not interested in wine. Can I go back now please?' She tried to pull away but he increased his grip until it was painful.

'Just a little further then you'll understand.'

He led her into a dark curved passageway. It was cold. Dust lay thick on the bottles either side of her.

'Hugo, if this is a joke, then I don't find it very funny.'

He paused and backed her against a rack. Leaning forward, he tried to kiss her, but she turned her head away.

Hugo grimaced. 'No, not in the mood? Well then, let me show you a very special vintage that Dad's kept under *lock* and key for you.' He fumbled in the pocket of his trousers and pulled out a bunch of keys. Fitting one into an old iron door in front of them, he unfastened it and threw it open.

In the light cast by the low-watt bulb hanging from the ceiling, she saw her father sitting on the edge of a mattress, hands limp at his side.

'Darcie!' he struggled to his feet. She ran to him and he drew her into a hug.

'Dad.' Bursting into tears, she put her head on his shoulder. He was dirty and unshaven, but he was alive.

'I'll leave you two alone for a moment, shall I?' said Hugo. 'I'd hate to spoil the family reunion.'

With that, he closed the door and turned the key.

14

'I thought you were with your mom, Darcie.' Michael Lock rocked his daughter to and fro, trying to comfort them both. 'What on earth are you doing here?'

'I was persuaded to stay – by your boss.'

Michael went very still as he absorbed this information. She felt his shoulders tense under his shirt. For the first time she could remember, he swore in her hearing.

'I'll kill them if I get out of this alive,' he muttered. Then glancing over to the door, he bent his head close to Darcie's ear. 'Say nothing. You know nothing.'

Darcie pulled away and looked into her father's hazel eyes. He flicked them to the door and to the wall behind her. She understood. They were probably watching to see what she said. But she had to risk telling him at least one thing.

'Uncle Ian came with me. You know you asked him to keep an eye on me.'

Michael Lock guided her to sit beside him on the mattress and put his arm around her. The stupid evening gown was too thin to offer any warmth in this cold place and she was shivering.

'How is the old rogue?' he asked her casually.

'Oh, you know, same as ever. Fit as a fiddle and forever climbing things. He went hunting this afternoon and I've not seen him since.'

This was madness. They were both trying to pretend that locking up your house guests was a perfectly ordinary end to the evening, to be dealt with by swapping family gossip while others listened in to their conversation.

'How's Mom?'

'She's in the States.'

'That's good.' He dropped his chin on to the top of his daughter's head. 'I'm very proud of you, Darcie, you know that? And I'm sorry – more sorry than I can say.'

'What do you think they'll do next?' She nestled close to him. Despite everything, it was just so good to touch him once more.

'With any luck they'll just leave us to stew while they get on with whatever they've got planned.'

Darcie sat up abruptly. 'No! We can't let them do that! What about –?' She was about to mention Kassim's name but her father put his hand over her mouth.

'Don't worry. I'm sure Tegla will remember to feed your dog. We just have to wait until they're ready to let us go.'

He was staring hard at her, willing her to follow his lead. She nodded slightly and he let go.

'Now, why don't you try and sleep? It's way past your bedtime.'

She half-laughed, half-sobbed to hear him say something so homely.

'OK, I'll try.' She put her head in his lap and he covered her with a blanket, stroking her hair as she closed her eyes. Darcie pretended not to notice the tears that were running silently down his face, dripping on to her bare shoulder.

*

Darcie did not know how many hours had passed when the door banged open. She had fallen asleep and now woke with a start. Her dad's arm was still resting on hers. The only move he made was to tighten his grip, determined not to be separated from her.

'You're both to come with me.' It was Hugo, flanked by two mercenaries, one with a gold earring, the other tall with short red hair.

Michael helped his daughter to her feet.

'OK?' he asked, his voice firm and confident.

Darcie tried to smile. 'Fine.' She kicked off her shoes and picked them up by the straps. 'No need to put myself through any more torture, is there?'

As soon as she said it, she realised how unfunny that was. Neither of them knew what the Krauses had planned. Whatever it was, she doubted it would be painless.

Prodded by the rifle barrel carried by the red-head, they followed Hugo back through the cellar tunnel and out into the courtyard. The house was quiet now. All the guests had departed – swallowed up by the night, safely on their way to Nairobi. The servants had cleared away the buffet and glasses. Only a few last candles guttered in their niches along the walls. Hugo led them into his father's study. Mr Kraus was sitting behind the desk; Madame Tsui was also standing looking out the window towards the glow of the city lights, cigarette holder in hand. The end glowed like a firefly dancing at her fingertips.

'Here they are, Dad,' said Hugo.

'Please sit down,' said Mr Kraus, gesturing to two chairs on the rug in front of him. A third chair stood empty. Michael squeezed her hand and they both sat, not letting go of each other. 'A very touching sight. Father and daughter together at last. I had wanted to bring it about earlier but the young lady had other ideas. We had to wait for her to walk into the lion's den of her own accord.'

'I'll tell you where the disk is. Just let her go,' said Michael determinedly.

'No, no, no. That doesn't matter now. Though, of course, it may make us feel more lenient towards you if you tell us, as we've thought of another use for that disk.'

Michael looked once at his daughter then back at Mr Kraus. It was his only card and he had to play it. 'It's in her schoolbag. No one will have found it there – Darcie doesn't even know it's there.'

'No?'

'Darcie isn't very tidy. She never empties that bag.'

'I see. You think you know your daughter well do you?'

Michael nodded.

'So you wouldn't be surprised to find out that she came here with a most unusual uncle.' Mr Kraus pushed a button on his desk, releasing the lock on the front door. Darcie heard boots and the sound of something being dragged across the hall. Two more mercenaries came in, carrying Stingo between them. He had been wounded in the leg and his hands were tied behind his back. He seemed barely conscious.

'Uncle Ian!' Darcie rushed to his side as they dumped him on the third chair, catching him before he fell off sideways. Michael came to his other side and helped her pull him up.

Stingo's eyes opened. He swore. 'Darcie, you shouldn't be here,' he said through swollen lips.

'Sit down, both of you,' rapped out Mr Kraus.

Neither of them moved. Hugo stepped forward and pulled Darcie away, forcing her back to her chair; a soldier gestured to Michael to do as he was told.

'I did tell you we had an entertaining hunt this afternoon,' Hugo said to Darcie with a smile like a knife slash, breath hot in her face. He was flushed with excitement, high on the diet of violence his father had been feeding him. 'Dear old Uncle Ian gave us very good sport, except for the fact that the cheat wore a bullet-proof vest. So you can stop pretending he's your uncle. He won't tell us – so it's up to you: who is he really, Darcie?'

'He's Ian Lock,' Darcie said steadily. She could feel her father stiffen beside her.

'That's rubbish, Darcie. There is no Ian Lock. He's British army, isn't he?'

Darcie bit her lip, wondering what she should say. Their only hope now was that the SAS teams would come for them but the one thing she must not do was betray the presence of any outsiders. What story would Hugo believe?

'OK, Hugo, you're right. He's not my real uncle. He's a bouncer from the Safari Club. We've been going out for a while now. I asked him to come to protect me from creeps like you.'

Hugo drew back, his mouth curling in an ugly sneer. 'Bit old for you, isn't he?'

'You should realise by now that I prefer the company of real men, Hugo, not spoilt rich boys.'

'You little –!' Hugo raised his hand.

'Enough!' It wasn't Mr Kraus who had spoken but Madame Tsui. She tapped her ash on to the floor. 'We have no time for this. We have the two men – that's all we need.' She walked over to Darcie's father and took his jaw in her long fingers, swivelling his head as if looking for his best side. He pulled away in revulsion. 'Tomorrow, after the tournament, Michael Lock will be paraded on national television as the corrupt official responsible for passing information about the security arrangements to the terrorists.' She blew a thin curl of smoke into his face. 'He will be the most reviled man in Britain by the time the Monday morning papers are printed.' She moved to Stingo and kicked him with her foot. 'His accomplice, this ex-army man here, whoever he is, will be shown to have provided the explosives. Fortunately for us, we have proof that he went to the Yaqoubi place on Tuesday – a perfect opportunity to give our young martyr the goods. They'll both have brief show trials then goodbye.' She turned back to Mr Kraus and smiled. 'First decisive action by our new president and no one will dare question him or complain that he doesn't do enough to crack down on terrorism.'

Mr Kraus took a swig of his whiskey. 'What about the girl? She's no danger to us, is she, if we keep her locked up for a while?'

Madame Tsui walked over to Darcie and lifted her chin with the tip of a long-nailed finger. 'Oh, but she is. If she's found, she makes them look innocent. Had we more time, I'd redeploy her elsewhere in my organisation. With a bit of re-education, she could be very useful. It is a shame to waste human resources.' Madame Tsui thought for a moment, making her own calculations. 'Unfortunately, time is against us. We'll have to get rid of her.' She turned her back and walked to the window. 'Take her out, shoot her and leave the lions to dispose of the body.'

Mr Kraus nodded. 'I've just the man for the job.'

'No!' Michael Lock burst up from his chair. Stingo staggered to his feet, ready to headbutt anyone in reach.

'Sit down or I'll order my son to kill her now in front of you,' barked Mr Kraus.

Michael looked round to see Hugo with a gun at his daughter's head. The boy looked as if he'd enjoy pulling the trigger. Darcie's eyes were wide with terror.

'Please, no! She's not important to you. She knows nothing. She's only fourteen for pity's sake!' Michael collapsed back on the chair. Stingo was kicked into his.

'Take her outside,' Mr Kraus gave his son a curt nod. 'Now.'

Michael and Stingo watched helplessly as Darcie was led away.

'I'm very sorry for the unpleasantness, Madame Tsui,' Mr Kraus said.

'Do not apologise. It is a necessary sacrifice.' She checked her watch. 'It is time we went to Nairobi. Search the girl's things in case the disk is there, then lock these two up again.' She gave Stingo a quick examination, taking in his bloodstained trousers, weakness and pale skin. 'Give this one something to keep him alive. He's lost too much blood already. Goodbye, gentlemen. I probably won't be seeing you again but I'll enjoy watching your trial.'

With that, Madame Tsui wrapped a fur around her shoulders and went out to her car. Mr Kraus stayed for a moment to give his men their orders, then followed her. Once they had left, the soldiers pulled their two prisoners to their feet.

'This way.' The red-head prodded the two men

towards Darcie's bedroom. 'You, on your knees.' The mercenary forced Stingo down while a second soldier kept a gun to his head. 'And you, tell us where this bag is.' He gestured to Michael to start looking. 'Any funny business and we shoot him.'

As a distraught Michael Lock searched the room under the eye of his captor, Stingo was trying to think of a plan. He could see the phone on the bed. Too far to reach. Then he saw the hairband on the floor, a small red light blinking on its underside indicating that the microphone was on. Thanking Darcie silently, he suddenly shouted out.

'They've got Darcie. They're going to. . .'

He got no further. A gun barrel thumped him on the back of the head. 'Shut it!' said the mercenary.

'The hard man's finally cracked,' sniggered the one with the gold earring.

His jeers were interrupted by the crackle of gunfire from away to the north. Silence fell in the room.

'It's too late. I'm sorry, Michael,' groaned Stingo.

Darcie's father collapsed on to the bed, hugging his daughter's pyjamas to his chest.

Up on the bluff, the SAS team burst into action. Midge radioed a brief message.

'We're going in. What's Zebra's last known position?'

Gladys went white but her voice remained calm. 'Her phone's still in her bedroom. The signal's not changed.'

Midge swore softly. 'But she could be anywhere. We're going to need backup. Merlin, radio to B-team to make their move. We'll rendezvous with the helicopter at the landing place.'

'How soon can you be there, captain?' asked Gladys.

'With the helicopter? An hour.'

'That may be too late for Darcie.'

Midge silently cursed Gladys and all her kind. 'I understand that, but I can't lead an effective rescue with two men. I have to have air support.'

'But, captain –!'

Midge couldn't stop himself. 'You were the one who said she was in no danger; you were the one who left her in there when Stingo wanted her out. We know Lock and Stingo are still alive – if we balls up this operation, they'll be dead too.'

'The helicopter's on its way, captain,' said Merlin.

'Roger that. Over and out.'

When Darcie was led away Hugo took her down to a garage at the back of the house and handed her over to two familiar men in a white Land Cruiser.

'It's my lucky day, boss,' leered the man with the gold bracelet. 'I get to finish the business.'

'Take her to the northern end of the estate and shoot her. No messing about – that's an order, Mickey,' Hugo said sternly. 'Make it quick and clean.'

'OK, boss,' grimaced Mickey.

'Leave the body for the animals to clean up. It's an accident, girl snatched by lion while out walking – got that?' Hugo turned back to Darcie. 'You know, I'm sorry about this, Darcie.'

'You're sorry?' How dare he! She turned her face from him. He reached over and pulled her head round, thumb tracing the line of her jaw.

'Yeah, well, I didn't think it'd go like this. I thought I might at least get a kiss.'

She slapped his hand away and told him what he could do with his kisses. He laughed.

'You've got guts – I like that. But your problem is you think like prey rather than like a hunter. Otherwise you would never've come here, even with your muscle-bound boyfriend in tow.'

'Look, if you're going to kill me, at least have the decency not to bore me to death first,' said Darcie through clenched teeth. She was terrified and furious. They meant to murder her and no one was close enough to stop them. Her voice shook but she refused to cry. 'I'll have my handbag, please.'

He fumbled in his pocket. 'What for? Are you worried about being eaten alive out there? Don't. I've asked them to make sure you're very dead when you become dinner for some lucky lion.'

She snatched the bag from him.

'Hugo, you are sick.'

'But you're terminal. Goodbye, Darcie.'

He tapped the roof of the vehicle. Darcie felt it surge forward as it pulled out of the yard and began the climb up the steep track behind the house.

Darcie had been put in the back. Her hands were unbound. She surreptitiously tried the door handle. Mickey saw her in the wing mirror and laughed.

'Child locks. Very useful for our younger passengers.'

She knew time was running out for her and she had only one idea. It might kill her, but she had nothing to lose. Reaching up behind her head, she pulled the seat belt over her chest and fastened it.

'Look at the kid!' mocked Mickey to his partner. The driver had dark glasses pushed up on his forehead. Darcie could see that his eyes were dilated as if he was on some kind of private trip. He probably was – this whole outfit had a surreal, drug-induced insanity to it. 'Nicely brought up girl – so safety conscious. I must remember to tell her dad when we get back.'

The car was swinging around the hairpin bends that wound above the house, headlamps raking the bushes like searchlights. She knew from the aerial shots she'd seen that the track headed over the shoulder of the hill down on to the plateau to the north. Darcie felt inside her clutch bag.

Quickly, she leant forward and sprayed the can over the driver. A stinging gas filled the compartment, blinding everyone, burning their throats. The car swerved and bucked, crashed through the bushes at the side of the road and rolled down an embankment. Men and weapons rattled around inside like peas in a can. Darcie knew she was going to die. Her head struck the side window. She hung upside down, then felt herself jolt back into her seat. The car had stopped. Opening her eyes cautiously, she saw Mickey had gone through the windscreen and lay sprawled on the bonnet. The driver was slumped over the wheel, head at a strange angle.

Just then, she didn't care if they were dead or not. It was enough that she was alive and had a chance to get out before either of them recovered. She unbuckled her seatbelt, relieved to find that she appeared to have escaped any major injuries, and crawled out through the smashed window. Mickey's gun lay on the ground beside his body. She picked it up, wondering what to do with it. She couldn't leave it in case he came round. Slinging it over her shoulder, she scrambled up the bank, cutting her bare feet on broken glass. That wouldn't do. She wouldn't get far without shoes. Ripping off the heels of Madame Tsui's designer footwear, she converted them into sandals and tied them around her ankles by their stout straps. Climbing again, she made it back to the road.

What now? A trickle of blood crept down her cheek from a cut on her temple. She felt as if she'd just crawled out of the washing machine having been put through the spin cycle. Back to the house? That would do no good. She would probably get caught and, besides, she knew that neither Stingo nor her father were in immediate danger. Kassim was the one she had to save now. She had to contact the High Commission or one of the SAS teams. The best plan would be to find the nearest phone and that meant reaching a village. If her memory served her well, the ridge ahead was the narrowest part of the three fences: the barriers were forced together to pass through a narrow gully. She might be able to climb over at that point.

Shakily, she began to trudge up the road. The way was lit by moonlight and she could see the red tyre-rutted earth quite clearly winding ahead of her. Mosquitoes whined in her ear, humming around the cut on the side of her face. She brushed them away. Her body was aching all over but she forced herself to continue. She did not have the luxury of time to allow herself to feel the full shock of what she had just been through.

Suddenly, turning a corner, she came to an abrupt halt. In the centre of the road stood a lion, as surprised to see her as she was to see it. The pupils of its eyes glowed in the moonlight, the thick fur of its mane was a dark smudge around its pale face. The lion stared at her, confused. Attracted by the enticing scent of blood further down the road, it had not anticipated a small human to come walking towards it. Was it prey or a hunter?

Darcie grabbed her gun. She squeezed the trigger into the air. Nothing happened.

'The safety catch,' she muttered, cursing her stupidity. Fumbling on the barrel, she found it and slid it back. Squeezing again, she let off a quick round into the sky. Bullets sprayed all over the place as she struggled with the unexpectedly powerful recoil. She'd never held a gun, let alone fired one before, and it showed. The lion turned and slipped into the bushes. Darcie didn't know if it was scared off or just disgusted at her incompetence. That didn't matter. It was gone – that was the main thing.

The road climbed steeply for the last hundred metres until Darcie came to the gully. The moon rode above the ridge, bathing the scene in pearly light. The dark shrieked with the maddening song of the cicadas, adding to her thumping headache. Pausing for breath, hands on her knees as she bent over, she thought she could hear gunfire behind her. Had the car been found? Was the pursuit on? She had to make her move at once before they caught up with her.

A quick examination of the fence told her that there was no way to cut through without tools. As for climbing, that too looked impossible. Her fingers bled from just touching one of the wires. She began to fear that she was trapped after all.

Then she saw it: the way out. Up the hill, the moonlight was glinting on a telephone pole. Wires connected it to a pole lower down the slope but on the other side of the fences. She'd seen something very like this before – the death slide.

'I am completely mad,' Darcie cursed as she struggled her way up the rocks to the post. Reaching behind her, she tore off the silk train of her dress and folded it into a loop. Tucking her shoes into her bodice, she threw the silk round the trunk and leaned back. Slowly, she edged her way up the pole like a boy climbing a coconut tree. She didn't allow herself to consider what would happen if she slipped. Silk is very strong, she told herself. Finest thread from Madame's own farms, it wouldn't dare let her down. Inching up, she climbed above the treetops. Finally, she reached the rests at the top of the pole, put there to support the engineer's ladder. Clinging to the wood for a moment, she looked down the slide before her. The wires individually were too thin to carry her. She'd have to use as many as she could to bear her weight and even then she'd need some kind of harness to slide down.

Pulling off one of her sandals, she tied the leather thong around four wires, using the slack to bunch them together. They sprang apart, putting strain on the shoe, but it held. Once further from the pole, the wires would be looser and she should be able to slide more easily. Next she threaded her silk remnant through the shoe and looped the ends round her wrists.

'Please God, keep me safe!' she muttered to the starry night sky, hoping someone up there was listening. She had to pray that Madame Tsui demanded high levels of craftsmanship from her shoemakers or this would be a very short trip.

She leapt forward into the void. First slowly, then

with gathering speed, she began to slide down the wires. The first fence was passed, then the second; she had to lift her legs to clear the third, then the finishing post loomed up. The spreading wires slowed her, but not enough. How was she going to stop?

Thump. That was how. Darcie collided with the pole and almost lost her grip. The world span before her eyes. She hugged the wood, just thankful for the moment to be alive. Her dizziness passing, Darcie hitched her legs over the metal rests to take a firmer seat. Next, she untied her makeshift harness, slid down the pole and touched ground. Somewhere over the hill, she could hear the throb of a helicopter engine. Fearing she was being tracked, she stumbled away as fast as she could into the dark.

15

06.00, Kiserian: Sunny with prospect of thunderstorms later.

Darcie walked into the garage at the roadside village of Kiserian at dawn. No one was serving, but a pay phone stood at the far end of the forecourt. She picked up the receiver and dialled the operator.

'Reverse charge call to the British High Commission, please,' she said.

The operator disappeared for a moment and then came back. 'I'm sorry, the High Commission does not accept reverse charge calls. The switchboard is closed. I can give you the emergency number if you want.'

'But I haven't got any money!'

'I'm sorry, then you'll have to call back when the High Commission opens on Monday and see if they'll take your call then.'

Darcie could hear the sound of a vehicle approaching the garage. Ducking out of the booth she saw a camouflaged jeep pull up at the pump. She didn't recognise the men, but she guessed that they must be part of the mercenary force from the farm. They seemed to be in a great hurry, shouting and yelling about something.

'Look, OK, I'll try someone else,' she said desperately to the operator. But whom? She dug in her clutch bag and pulled out a business card, stuffed in there absent-mindedly a week ago. 'Can you try Jordan's Jolly Taxi Service, Nairobi 55 67 03. Tell him it's Darcie.'

While Darcie waited, the men banged on the door of the garage and roused the owner. Angry voices accompanied the reluctant filling of their tank.

'Putting you through now.'

'Thank you, God,' breathed Darcie, leaning her head against the phone. 'Thank you.'

'*Jambo*, Jolly Taxis here –'

'Jolly, it's me – Darcie.'

She heard a resigned sigh. 'Are you in trouble again, sister?'

'Yes – much worse than last time,' she sobbed, so grateful to hear his cheerful voice on the other end. '*Kali*, very, very *kali*.'

'That bad, huh? I come and get you, *sawa*?'

'Please hurry. I'm really, really grateful.' Darcie quickly told him her whereabouts. 'I'll wait behind the kiosk on the corner. Pull into the garage and I'll come to you.'

'I'll be there as soon as I can.'

'And Jolly?'

'Yeah? Don't tell me – you have not got any money.'

'No, but I'll pay you I promise when we get back to Nairobi.'

'*Hakuna matata*, sister. Let us get you home in one piece first.'

Darcie tried to look inconspicuous behind the kiosk but the presence of a white girl in evening dress could not be kept from the curious children of Kiserian. A little boy found her about half an hour later. He stared at her with his wide chocolate coloured eyes and ran back into his house. He returned with his sister who carried a cup of water unsteadily over the rocky earth.

'How are you, lady?' the girl asked in her best primary school English.

Darcie gave a shaky smile. 'Fine, thanks. Can I have some?' She pointed to the cup.

The girl handed it to her solemnly. 'You do not look fine. Shall I fetch Mama?'

Another jeep roared by, radio squawking and fizzing. Gun fire popped faintly in the distance.

'No, no, I'm just hiding – playing hide and seek. Don't give me away will you?'

'Who are you hiding from?'

'Those bad men in the cars.'

The girl seemed to accept this as a perfectly reasonable explanation.

'Have they counted to ten? Are they coming to find you?'

'Yes, that's right. So say nothing about me, *sawa*?'

'*Sawa*.' The girl turned to her brother and translated the explanation into their local language, Kikuyu.

Darcie tried to smile at the little boy but she found she couldn't summon up a reassuring expression. She wiped her forehead, coming away with blood on the back of her hand.

The girl frowned. 'Your head is bad. Are you sure you do not want Mama? You can come to our house: she will be back soon.'

Darcie hesitated for a moment. If she stayed out in the open, she'd be spotted by hostile eyes sooner rather than later. It was worth the risk.

'OK. Thanks, I'd like that.'

She followed the two children into a small dwelling just off the road. A well-trodden path wound between the family's fruit trees to a white-washed house. Chickens pecked on the little wooden veranda. A flock of Superb starlings in their bright coats of orange and blue fought over some sprinkled grains of maize. It was very dark inside the house and it took a moment for her eyes to adjust. The floor of the single room was made of beaten earth, the roof from corrugated tin. The family's few possessions were neatly stacked on shelves out of reach of the ants that claimed ownership of anything left on the ground. A cheap notebook and stubby pencil lay on a stool just inside the door.

'No school today?' asked Darcie.

'It is Sunday,' the girl said simply.

Of course, Sunday. The day of the polo match.

Darcie collapsed on to a wooden bench and closed her eyes. She mustn't fall asleep. She had to ignore her pounding head and exhaustion. Jolly would be here soon.

The smell of ripe fruit roused her from her half-doze. The boy had put some bananas into her lap as his sister held out a warm coke in a thick glass bottle. Darcie downed everything gratefully.

'Thank you. Where's your mama gone?'

'To take Papa his food. He is in hospital. Very sick.'

Darcie was struck with guilt as she realised she was probably eating the best that the house had to offer. She felt she had to give them something in return so she handed the girl her clutch bag – it was empty, but it was all that she had on her now.

'Here, have this.'

The girl's face lit up. 'So pretty!'

'I'm glad you like it. It's yours.'

They all looked up as they heard the car crunch on to the forecourt of the garage. The girl put her head out of the window.

'Who is it?' Darcie asked fearfully.

'A taxi. Is it for you?'

Darcie felt a huge surge of relief. Tears sprung into her eyes but this time she did manage to smile. 'Yes. It's my friend, he's come to find me.'

'You want this man to find you?'

'Yes, he's not one of the bad ones. You won't say that you found me, will you, if anyone asks?'

The two children shook their heads.

'Thank you.'

Darcie got up and ran to the taxi, throwing herself into the front seat.

'Please get me out of here,' she gasped as she waved to the two children staring curiously at her from their front door.

'Where to?' asked Jolly, looking very unlike his name as he saw the state of her. He reversed out of the garage and turned back towards Nairobi.

'What time is it?'

'About eight.'

The tournament was this morning. She did not know exactly when play was to start – early probably to escape the midday sun. That meant everyone she needed to talk to would be there and not at the High Commission.

'Can you drive me to the Country Club?'

'I should be driving you to a hospital, sister. What has happened to you?'

'I suppose you could say I've been a fashion victim.' She gave a shuddering laugh, on the edge of hysteria. 'Will you take me?'

'Of course I will take you. I am your knight in shining armour. I do what my lady asks.'

'Thanks, Jolly.'

'Here.' He reached behind him and handed her his jacket. 'Put this on.'

She pulled the too-large sleeves over her arms and lay with her throbbing head against the windowpane.

'There are some sweets in the dashboard if you want something,' he added.

Getting no answer, he turned to his passenger and saw that she was fast asleep. Shaking his head, he put his foot down and let the car eat up the miles back to Nairobi.

Kassim checked the tack of his pony carefully. The straps were fine – everything just as it should be. He next examined his kit in the mirror by the changing rooms, yeah, he was ready. Boots polished, jodhpurs spotless – he'd do. He wondered for a brief moment if Darcie was going to be in the crowd. He'd have to look out for her.

Hugo Kraus walked through the waiting ponies and riders, greeting everyone with his usual casual charm.

'All right, Kassim? Got everything you need?'

Kassim nodded.

'There's one last security check to do on the ponies,

then you can go out to the pitch.' Hugo held out his hand.

'Another check?' grumbled Kassim. He'd been searched several times already that morning. The British police protecting the prince had been very thorough.

'Yeah, bit of a bore, but there you are. That's the cost of playing with royalty.'

'I s'pose.' Kassim relinquished the reins of his pony to Hugo. The older boy turned to go. 'Er, Hugo, did you bring Darcie with you?'

Hugo paused, then turned back, a strange smile on his face. 'No.'

'I thought she was with you this weekend?'

'Yeah, she was, but she went to bed late – couldn't get up in time to be here. I bet she'll be sorry tomorrow she missed it.'

'I doubt it,' Kassim said sullenly.

'Oh, I almost forgot: she said to wish you a special "good luck".' Hugo's smile was chilling; for the first time, Kassim felt worried.

'She's OK, isn't she? Nothing's happened to her, has it?'

'There's nothing for you to worry about. She's fine now. Come on, boy.' Clicking his tongue, he led the pony off to the security guard who stood with a metal detector by the entrance to the pitch.

Fine now? So did that mean she hadn't been before? Kassim shook his head, wishing he could call her, but he didn't even have her number. As soon as the match was over, he'd find a way of contacting her – just to check.

'Hey, Darcie, wake up. I cannot get any closer.'

Darcie blearily rubbed her eyes as Jolly shook her shoulder gently. She felt worse, if anything, now she'd had a rest. Given the choice, she'd sleep for a week.

'There seems to be something going on. We have to park here,' he explained, turning into a field full of four-wheel drives. Brightly dressed ladies wearing big hats were tottering over the rutted grass accompanied by men in blazers and ties. The Country Club was festooned with green and yellow bunting, white marquees shone in the sun.

'It's the polo tournament,' Darcie said, her heart sinking. Everything looked normal – which meant that the SAS had not got here yet. Where were they? Were they still watching the farm, thinking she was just having a lie-in? Well, if the SAS didn't know what was afoot, that meant no one else yet knew what Tsui and the Krauses had planned. It was down to her.

She looked towards the club. Banners over the road proclaimed that the first chukka was to begin at ten-fifteen. 'What time is it?'

'Nearly ten.'

Sleep forgotten, Darcie was already out of the car when Jolly caught up with her.

'What are you doing?' he asked her, seizing her elbow.

'Trying to prevent a disaster.'

'Darcie, that blow to your head must be making you think funny. This is just a polo match.'

'Look, Jolly,' she said, shaking him off. 'You don't know me as anything but a crazy girl who keeps getting into trouble, I understand that, but please trust me. We've got to tell the organisers not to go ahead.

We must tell them at all costs to stop Kassim al Yaqoubi going on to the pitch with the others, can you remember that?'

'Kassim who?' Jolly was scratching his head, totally bemused by all this.

Darcie felt like screaming but she had to keep calm. 'Kassim al Yaqoubi. There's a bomb planted on his saddle. A bunch of extremist nutters are trying to blow up the British prince who's playing in the tournament. Now do you get it?'

'OK.' Jolly drew his oily palm over his forehead. 'I get it – I think.'

Darcie's mind was now in overdrive as she sorted through their options. 'You go towards the stand over there – find one of the officials or a security guard. Tell them Darcie and Michael Lock sent you. Ask to speak to someone from the High Commission if they make trouble. I'll go to the club house to see if I can find anyone.'

Jolly Jordan started to move off into the crowds, doubtless thinking life would have been much simpler if he'd refused the reverse charge call.

'And one more thing, Jolly,' Darcie called after him. 'If play starts, get away from the pitch. Take as many people with you as you can persuade to leave.'

'And how am I do that, sister?'

'I dunno. Shout "bomb" I suppose.'

With a resigned shrug at the insanity he'd been plunged into, Jolly strode rapidly off towards the public entrance. Darcie headed for the club house. She could see a huge lorry parked among the refreshment tents beyond it. The vehicle was the kind she'd only ever seen before as part of a travelling circus. *Tsui's World of Fashion* was written on the side in blood red lettering. She wondered with a brief flicker of satisfaction what the designer would make of the alterations Darcie had seen fit to make to a central piece in her latest collection.

Ducking into the shadow of the rear wall of the Country Club, Darcie took stock of her situation. It was a building she knew well. Lying outside the security cordon around the polo pitch, she thought she might be able to get into it through the gym where she practised her fencing; the fire door was often left wedged opened to keep it cool. The organisers would probably be using part of the club house to coordinate the event – it would be as good a place as any for her to raise the alarm. She had to get to someone in authority first before the Krauses spotted her.

Her luck was in: thanks to the last overheated weight-lifter, she was able to slip in the gym without having to risk the front entrance. There was no one using the equipment now and she thought she had a clear run to the corridor beyond. She was about to congratulate herself on the successful completion of the first stage of her plan when someone entered from the other end, walking calmly towards her.

'My, my,' said Hugo Kraus. 'You don't die easily, do you? I must say I was surprised to see you on the CCTV. Not a ghost, are you?'

'No thanks to you,' said Darcie. She looked desperately for a way round him. She moved to the side wall; he changed course to intercept.

'You forgot that this is a major security operation, Darcie. Dad, as one of the Club House Committee, is on security, of course, keeping a close eye on who turns up. I believe some mad Kenyan has already been stopped at the gate shouting something about a bomb. He didn't seem too clear on the details, but no doubt a night in the cells will help him regain his senses.'

Darcie edged past the rowing machine. 'You're not going to get away with this.'

'Oh, I think we will. Once we've dealt with you. Dad said it would be good character-building stuff if I had that pleasure.'

Darcie heard a click. Hugo held a gun pointing directly at her. Sweat trickled down her back as the moment seemed to last an eternity.

She finally found her voice. 'Go on, shoot. If you do, you'll have every policeman for miles running in here. How will you explain your murder of an unarmed girl?'

Hugo smiled. 'True. Thank you for reminding me.' He slid the safety catch on and tucked the gun into his back pocket. 'I'll have to do it the hard way then. I know how, you know.' He cracked his knuckles, his eyes lingering on her bare neck.

'You're sick, Hugo. Your dad should be locked up – he's turned you into a monster.' The ropes on the wall swung lazily as she brushed by.

'No, he's made me into a soldier – a hunter. You, my dear Darcie, are going to learn what it means to be a hunter's prey.'

'You are so full of bull, Hugo.'

Darcie finally reached the rack of fencing blades she'd been edging towards. She grasped her favourite sword and pulled it out, holding it in the guard position, at the same time wriggling out of the encumbrance of Jolly's over-large jacket.

'What's this!' Hugo was delighted by this development. 'You're going to fight? Brilliant. This is going to be fun.' He lunged towards the rack and grabbed the nearest blade.

Made for sport rather than life-threatening situations, the foils were flexible and blunt, but as neither of them was padded up, Darcie knew she could probably inflict enough punishment to keep him off until she made it into the corridor. If pushed, she could go for his eyes but she was reluctant to start a fight that she knew would probably result in injuries.

'Let me past,' snarled Darcie.

'I'd like to see you try.'

That was it. Darcie launched herself at Hugo, dealing him a flurry of efficient strikes to keep him on the defensive so he had to back up the hall. His eyes widened in alarm as he struggled to defend himself, surprised by her unexpected skill with the blade. Had Darcie been at full strength and properly dressed, she could've made it out of the gym, but her disintegrating sandals caught on a mat and she stumbled.

'Wow, Darcie, I'm impressed,' said Hugo. He lunged for the attack, displaying that he too had had lessons with the major. A wild slash hit one of the ropes behind her, sending it into a mad dance. The backswing hit her and in that instant, Hugo whipped the blade across the flesh of her upper arm, leaving a welt like a stroke from a cane. She yelped.

He paused to grin at her. 'Give up, Darcie? Why don't you let me end this now?'

She backed off, heading towards the changing rooms, still parrying his thrusts. Reaching the swing door, she pushed backwards through it, using the few seconds that bought her to dive behind one of the benches.

The door was kicked open.

'Come, come, Darcie, you can't think to take sanctuary in the ladies' changing room. That's not going to stop me killing you.'

Hugo began to patrol the racks of pegs, tapping his sword on the wire mesh. Darcie crawled to the last aisle and slumped in the corner, cradling her arm. She was almost at the end of her strength. Part of her was saying it would be easier just to give up now. She screwed up her eyes, willing herself to make one final effort.

'Oh, Darcie, you can't run, you know. A good hunter can always follow a trail, particularly when the prey is tired and beaten,' said Hugo gleefully, turning into the far end of the aisle. 'Aw, all washed up, are we? Had enough? You know, Darcie, I wish I could keep you alive – I do love playing with you. Just think of the fun we could have out on the farm.'

Loathing for this maniac gave her the burst of energy that she needed. Seizing a tennis racket from a sports bag on the bench beside her in her left hand, she got to her feet, her blade still steady in her right.

'Anyone for tennis?' mocked Hugo.

He lunged towards her. She thrust the tennis racket forward. His blade passed through it, striking the wall behind her. Throwing herself sideways, she used the racket to trap his sword as she kicked the hilt from his grip. She recovered immediately to whip him across the face with her own blade. He instinctively covered his eyes. Darcie used that moment to land a kick to his groin. He doubled up with a high-pitched scream. Dropping her sword, she grabbed a bathrobe from a peg and threw it over his head and shoulders. Next she wrapped a pair of tights around his neck to hood him and kneed him again for good measure. He slumped to the floor.

'You've blinded me!' he said with a muffled cry of pain, hysterical now as he flailed around trying to grab her.

Knocking his feet from under him with a hockey stick, she knelt on his back, yanked his arms and tied his hands behind with a belt salvaged from the kitbag. He almost managed to dislodge her but finally she restrained him with a pair of tights to secure his ankles and a tennis skirt wrapped tightly around his knees.

Panting, she sat up. 'You got it wrong, Hugo. Not "anyone for tennis?" but "new balls please"!'

'I can't breathe!' screamed Hugo from within the folds of the towel.

'Yes, you can – if you lie still, relax, look pretty. Someone will find you – eventually.'

Ripping the gun out of his back pocket, Darcie went into the toilets and dropped it in the sanitary bin, figuring this was the last place he would look for it. Then picking up the two swords, she stumbled out of the changing room, through the gym and out into the corridor.

*

A tannoy crackled overhead.

'And here they are, Ladies and Gentlemen, taking their warm-up circuit of the pitch. First on to the field are our visitors, the Windsor Quartet, closely followed by our own Country Club Crusaders.' Applause rippled in through the open windows of the club house veranda.

Dumping the swords in an umbrella stand, Darcie gave up any thought of trying to find someone to stop the tournament. It would take too long to convince them she wasn't a crank; she'd have to do it herself. At the very least, she'd have to disrupt play so that they called a halt. The nearest entrance was the ticket checkpoint guarded by serious-looking security operatives with guns on their hips. She could see no sign of any of the SAS soldiers she'd met, nor any familiar faces from the High Commission. No good. To her right, she saw an encampment of horseboxes. Stable boys were chatting to each other while they held the spare horses ready for the next chukka.

Darcie recognised one of them and knew he was not likely to have forgotten her.

'The bell sounds and play begins,' continued the commentator. 'His Royal Highness takes immediate command of the ball with an excellent headshot. Millington intercepts. Good hook there from Yaqoubi. Yaqoubi in possession.'

Darcie ran over to Kassim's stable boy. He was holding the mount she'd ridden only last Tuesday. The man looked at her warily, his hand reflexively moving to protect his stomach. She knew she wouldn't inspire confidence in him as she was wearing a ripped dress, dripping blood from recent cuts, and covered in dust. It was too late for words. Slowing to a walk, she approached the stable boy with what she hoped was a disarming smile.

'Excuse me.' Striking like a snake, she snatched the reins from his hand, swung up on to the pony's back and spurred it forward. The man made a grab for her but he only came away with one very battered sandal. The horse sensed she meant business and for once was obeying her faultlessly. Darcie charged towards the barrier. It was closed. They were going to have to leap it.

'Yah!'

Surprised by the fierce kick to his flank, the pony jumped clear and thundered on to the polo pitch. This was more like it. He knew what to do now. He had to go straight towards where all those men with sticks were chasing the white thing on the ground.

A player at the rear of the pack spotted the invasion only as Darcie drew level with him. Putting surprise to her advantage, she seized the mallet from his hand and continued her charge into the melee. People in the crowd were yelling. The commentator was saying something about 'outrageous behaviour'. Darcie rode past a rider in the middle of the pack with a very familiar face, blue eyes and sandy hair, but ignored him. She headed directly for Kassim who was still intent on the ball. Only at the last moment did he look up, horror-struck as a mallet whistled through the air, hitting him in the back and catapulting him from his saddle. Casting the mallet aside, Darcie lunged for the reins of Kassim's horse, guided her own mount round and galloped the two ponies off the field towards the refreshment tents.

Zigzagging among the guy ropes to throw off pursuit, Darcie finally stopped, slid off her horse and gave it a slap on the rump to make it leave. Kassim's mount tried to follow, but Darcie caught its head.

'Easy now. Let's take a look at you.'

Her heart still pounding, Darcie tried to take calm movements so as not to alarm the sweating beast. She felt under the saddle at the front. Nothing. Lifting the leather flap on the left side, she found it – a flat disk-like object attached to the underside where it was difficult to see. On the face was a winking dial. 55. What? Minutes? No. The counter was running down even as she watched. 50 . . . 49 . . . The pony went very still, sensing its life depended on the strange creature at its side. It looked at her with one trusting brown eye. Darcie knew she had not a hope of disarming the bomb – that kind of stunt belonged to the movies. She'd blow them both up if she tried.

Taking a deep breath she wrenched the device from the saddle and ran towards the first thing with solid walls she could see – Tsui's World of Fashion. She bounded up the wooden gangway.

35, 34, 33.

A woman was standing at the top watching her. Darcie came to a halt. It was Madame Tsui.

'I was wrong about you,' the Chinese woman said coldly. 'You are extraordinarily resourceful.'

'Get out of my way.' Darcie couldn't believe the woman, standing so calmly with a bomb metres away from her. 'This is about to go off.'

'Give it to me. I'll disarm it.' Madame Tsui held out her hand.

20, 19, 18.

Darcie hesitated. Then, 'I don't trust you. You might throw it at the spectators down there – still create your disaster.'

'True, I might.' Madame Tsui smiled. 'But do you really want to die, Darcie? You will if you don't trust me.'

10, 9, 8.

'Forget it. Catch!'

Darcie threw the bomb like a frisbee over Madame Tsui's head and in through the open door of the exhibition trailer. With a look of horror, Madame Tsui watched it fly past her. It hit the floor with a clunk, skittering further in among the priceless silks and satins of the summer collection, then . . .

Boom!

The trailer exploded. Thrown from the steps by the force of the blast, Darcie crashed into the canvas wall of a marquee. The last thing she remembered was a searing pain – then nothing.

16

12.00, Nairobi: Early gloom to lift, replaced by sunny spells.

A shiny red heart bobbed in front of her amid a bank of flowers. Vision still blurred, Darcie closed her eyes again. Where was she? There were clean sheets under her, soft sounds outside of people talking and laughing, the blip of a machine, a breeze rippling the curtain.

'Darcie, are you awake?'

She opened her eyes once more. 'Dad?' She tried to turn but her head wouldn't obey.

'You're in hospital, Darcie. They've immobilised your neck because you hurt your spine with your last bit of heroics.'

Michael Lock appeared between her and the heart-shaped balloon. He looked tired but otherwise unharmed.

'You got out,' she whispered.

'Yes. Largely thanks to that remarkable bag of yours.

Saved me from a bullet more than once.'

'And Mom? Does she know?'

Michael nodded. 'She's furious, of course. On her way to meet us as I speak.'

'And Stingo?'

'In worse shape than me but better than you, I'd say.'

'What's wrong with me?'

'Broken arm, broken leg, whiplash to the neck, cuts, minor burns and bruises. You'll live, darling.'

Darcie closed her eyes again. She felt as if she was floating above her bed, not really attached to her much-abused body.

'How many painkillers am I on?' she mumbled.

'The entire medicine cabinet,' said Michael, patting her unbroken arm.

'Tell me what happened.'

Michael sat down at her bedside. 'Well, until you arrived on the pitch, all eyes were on the Krauses' place. The SAS moved in but had major difficulty extracting us from the house as they first had to get past the private army. Stingo and I were holed up in your room along with two of Kraus's men who were ripping your things apart. They couldn't get into your bag – it was driving them mad. Once the shooting started, it all got very hairy. It was only when the SAS finally reached us that we were able to alert them to the threat at the tournament. By then, it would've been too late if you hadn't got there first: they'd never've arrived in time. They radioed in and discovered the whole place in an uproar. A female streaker had assaulted a player on the pitch and then been involved in an explosion in the exhibition hall, completely destroying a priceless collection of clothes.' He chuckled. 'The Kenyans were trying both to arrest you and cart you off to the local hospital all at the same time. We had no idea it was you, of course. I . . . er . . . I was convinced you were dead, so was Stingo. It was only thanks to the insistence of a very pleasant chap called Jolly Jordan that the British High Commissioner got involved. He recognised you at once and ordered that you be brought to this hospital where we are now.'

'Good old Jolly.' Darcie tried to smile but found it too painful.

'Jo Kraus was arrested immediately. Apparently they had some difficulty finding the son at first and thought he'd fled. It wasn't until a thorough sweep of the building was carried out that they found him tied up in various items of ladies' underwear in the changing rooms, half-suffocated by a towelling robe. You didn't have anything to do with that, I suppose?'

'He tried to kill me.' Darcie's voice cracked. She wouldn't forget Hugo's relentless hunt for her in a hurry.

'I know, love. That boy is seriously damaged goods. I don't know what can be done for him. Anyway, both he and his father are in the hands of the Kenyan authorities now and not our problem.'

'And Madame Tsui?'

A light tap of heels over tiles made Darcie jump. She thought for one sickening moment that the woman was here with her. Michael Lock laid his hand on his daughter's.

'It's Agent Smith, Darcie. She asked to be here for

your debrief. She's come, I hope, to say sorry.'

Gladys Smith appeared in view, carrying a small box.

'Sorry?' Gladys raised an eyebrow. 'To have you alive, a plot foiled and one part of a smuggling ring closed down? I think not.'

Michael shook his head but Darcie thought she had a point.

'To answer your question, Darcie,' continued Gladys, 'our Ringmaster, Madame Tsui, was removed from the scene by her people before the truth about her was known, leaving us with just the clowns, I'm afraid. We believe she was injured – how badly we do not know. If you're anything to go by – and it appears she was closer to the blast – then she'll not be in good shape. She was whisked away in a private ambulance and is no longer in East Africa. Gone to lick her wounds somewhere, I expect. She will not be pleased that her business venture here failed so spectacularly. She had hoped to have the government in her pocket so she could run her empire without scrutiny. That's all gone up in smoke along with her latest collection.'

'And Pearl?'

'Oh, the niece? Gone with her, I expect. The house is deserted.'

So she was too late. While she'd been lying out cold in a hospital bed, Pearl had obediently followed her employer to some new country, spared one stupid farmer to end up with another some day.

'Can we trace her?'

'Not unless we find Tsui. Why do you ask?'

'She was . . . we are friends.'

Her father sighed. 'Gladys, I told you that we shouldn't use Darcie to get near the girl. It's too messy – too personal.'

'But you told me Dad had suggested using me!' Darcie accused Gladys.

'I said we discussed it – which is true.'

'Discussed and rejected,' added Michael hotly.

'The point is that it worked.'

'The point is that my daughter's got hurt.'

A brittle silence stretched between them.

'Look, Dad, I agreed to help. I could've left if I

wanted,' Darcie said, feeling very tired of arguments. 'Can we just leave it? Tell me about the Yaqoubis.'

'You can see Kassim al Yaqoubi and ask him yourself,' said Gladys. 'He's in a room down the corridor with a broken collarbone and mild concussion, but has requested to see you when you are fit enough.

'I'll leave you two alone now. But before I go, let me give you this, Darcie. It might amuse you.' She handed over a folded magazine. 'Rest assured: the prince knows the full story. Also, he asked me to give you this.' She put the box in Darcie's palm.

The door opened to let Gladys out, giving Darcie a glimpse of a familiar armed guard outside. Michael smoothed out the copy of *Hello!* magazine and chuckled.

'I see what she means.' He held up the front cover which had a blurred picture of Darcie riding across the polo field, mallet in hand. *'Prince's groupies go polo loco!'* said the caption. *'Prince-mania reached alarming proportions in Nairobi, Kenya, on Sunday when an ardent admirer invaded the pitch in a misguided attempt to get close to the prince. The girl was later arrested.'*

'I'm under arrest, am I? Is that why Merlin's on the door?'

'Of course not. Fortunately for us, journalists never get things right. He's there because we are afraid of reprisals from one of Tsui's operatives. Neither of us are very popular in that quarter. Which means, Darcie, that as soon as you are fit to move, we are out of here for good. We're going to helicopter you to HMS *Invincible*, which is the closest Royal Navy vessel, and then from there we are disappearing from all radar screens, including, we hope, Madame Tsui's.'

'We?'

'The Lock family – you, me and Mom.'

'But what about my friends here?'

Michael walked to the window and fiddled with the blind cord.

'Darcie, you have to accept that you will not be allowed to see any of them again.'

'But Winston thinks you're a corrupt official and my

school mates all think I went mental and tried to attack a prince!'

'That's the price we have to pay for the life your mother and I chose. I know you didn't choose it but that's the way things are – you're reaping the consequences of our actions. You know, I suppose, that we should never've had you?'

Darcie blinked away the tears gathering in her eyes. 'I know.'

He turned to face her. 'Then I think you should also know that we had you because we were in love. We so desperately wanted a child we could love together. As two undercover agents, working for two different governments, it was wrong. We feared that a day like this would come, but we were selfish enough to go ahead anyway. Can you forgive us?'

She couldn't blame them for allowing her to exist. 'Yes.'

'Thank you.' Michael cleared his throat. 'Now, aren't you going to see what's in that box?'

He opened it for her and held up a gold pendant in

the shape of a polo horse and rider. It was inscribed: *With thanks to my favourite groupie. HRH.*

The following day, the doctors said it would be safe for her to sit up if she wore a neck support. Darcie felt much better now she was no longer immobilised on her back, though she quickly bored of *Hello!* and wondered what she could do to pass the time. She wasn't left wondering long because, as soon as breakfast was cleared away, Stingo barged into the room, propelling himself along in a chair. If wheelchairs could screech to a halt, this one would have done as he reached her bedside.

'Darcie Lock, you are the most impossible girl I've ever known. There I was, convinced you were dead, and the next thing I know you *are* almost dead but somewhere else! I am never going to accept an assignment as a bodyguard again.'

'Good to see you too, Stingo,' she smiled.

'My effing mates balls up the rescue thinking you were trapped up there somewhere. They were so busy blowing holes in the Kraus place looking for you that no one but the normal police protection squad were on hand to look after HRH, leaving it to some daft chick with a polo mallet.'

'I'm fine, thanks for asking.'

'Then that Tsui witch gets away as the Kenyans are preoccupied with the attempt to arrest you, so to top everything you're never going to be safe anywhere in the world, meaning I'm never going to stop worrying about you.'

'I didn't know you cared.'

'Of course I damn well care.' He stopped short.

'Is that a blush?' teased Darcie.

'Of course not.'

'No, you're a trained killer – you don't blush.'

He glared at her. 'And what was going on with the underwear thing in the changing room, Darcie?' he countered. 'Why didn't you just run him through?'

'That would be because I'm *not* a trained killer, Stingo.'

'No, thank God, you're not – or none of us would be

safe.' Having let out his torrent of words, Stingo finally gave her a smile. He reached out to ruffle her hair. 'Hell, it's good to see you alive. I wouldn't want to live through those hours after they took you away again.'

Nor would she.

'Thanks for the balloon, by the way,' said Darcie.

'It's from me and the lads. Like it or not, you're our unlucky mascot, Zebra.'

'I'm flattered.'

'We're not. It's back to basic training for us all, I expect. At least I can pass on a thing or two about bagpipes, shoes and tights.'

'You're not really in trouble for the way the operation went, are you?'

He laughed. 'No. It wasn't a bad outcome – saved the original man as ordered, took out the mercenaries, didn't lose our girl despite our best efforts to muck things up, no, we're not too unhappy. But what's going to happen to you now?'

'I'm not sure. Even if I knew, I probably wouldn't be able to tell you.'

He nodded. 'I s'pose not. Well, if ever I hear of a mad teenager causing trouble, I'll know where to find you.'

Kassim was her next visitor. She came out of a doze after lunch to find him sitting at her bedside staring at her. He had a large dressing on his forehead and his arm in a sling.

'Kassim,' she said sleepily.

'Darcie, how did you know about the bomb?' The question had clearly been weighing on his mind. She couldn't blame him.

She struggled to sit up. 'What have you been told?'

'I've been told that the Krauses were trying to set me up – something to do with that government minister they've arrested. They told me I would've been killed if it hadn't been for you.'

'Yeah, well. I had to do something, didn't I? The school football team wouldn't be the same without you.'

'But how did you know?'

She shrugged. 'I overheard Mr Kraus talking about it when I was out at their place this weekend.'

'Lucky for me you did.' He looked down at his hands. 'They say you're going away later today.'

'So I've been told.'

'Will you keep in touch?'

Darcie swallowed. 'I can't.'

'Why not?'

'It's complicated.'

'Try me.'

'I've made some enemies. I've got to vanish for a bit.'

Summoning the courage, he dared to take her hand and stroked it. Darcie felt a thrill of pleasure as she realised he really did like her.

'You've also made some friends,' he said softly. 'Let me know the moment you're allowed to re-materialise, won't you?'

'I will.' Even as she said it, she knew with a terrible sadness that time would never come. The unfairness of it all made her want to cry.

Kassim got up and leaned over the bed. 'Goodbye for now.' He kissed her gently. 'I wish we'd had more time.'

He closed the door behind him.

'So do I,' murmured Darcie, feeling the tears run down her cheeks.

Darcie and her father were driven by ambulance directly on to the runway at Wilson Airport where an RAF helicopter was waiting. Even though she was eager to see her mom who was already on the aircraft carrier, Darcie felt as if a lead weight was dragging at her – it seemed so wrong to slip away leaving her friends behind without a word of explanation. Her father had said that he'd made sure Tegla had been employed by another family; at least that meant Winston's school fees would get paid. But she'd never had a chance to thank Jolly after all he'd done for her.

Michael tapped her shoulder as the medics stretchered her out of the vehicle. 'I know I shouldn't have done it, but I couldn't take you away without letting you say goodbye. After all, you never chose this.' Her father nodded towards a tall Kenyan waiting on the hot tarmac.

'Jolly!' she cried.

Mr Jolly Jordan, mechanic, taxi driver and hero, walked over to the stretcher. Behind him, the familiar stubby skyline of Nairobi punctured the horizon, a brief interruption to the sweep of the African plains.

'Hey there, Darcie. You were not so mad after all,' he said, shaking her hand.

'I dunno – I was pretty loco to do what I did.' She smiled at him framed against the cloudless blue sky. 'Look after yourself, won't you?'

'I will. And Darcie?'

'Yeah?'

'If you need another taxi, just give me a ring – I will be there, *sawa*?'

'I might even pay you next time,' she grinned.

'I do not believe you. Ring anyway. Come back soon. *Safari mzuri!*'

Michael Lock shook hands with Jolly then signalled for the medics to load the stretcher on the helicopter. Jolly retreated to the car as the blades began to rotate. Grass bent in the wind; red dust swirled into the air, obscuring the window and hiding Kenya from her sight. Darcie lay down on the stretcher. She was never going back.

15.00, SIS Headquarters, London: Cooler night than of late with some mist and fog patches.

A file bearing the title 'Ringmaster' lay open on the director's desk. Gladys Smith sat perfectly still now she had delivered her report, watching the man in front of her like a cat at a mousehole.

'So the family are now on board the aircraft carrier?' he asked, smoothing his club tie.

'Yes, sir.'

He tapped the file thoughtfully. 'Of course, none of this happened. Darcie was never involved.'

'That's right, sir. Would you like me to destroy all records of her involvement with us – personnel file and so on?'

Christopher Lock swung in his chair and gazed out at the tower of Big Ben across the river. He didn't want to show his relief that his son was safe, not even to his most trusted colleague. He'd bent every rule to get Michael out – a sign of his emotional weakness – and it had worried him that he had put his granddaughter at risk. Yet today, looking at the sun shining on the Thames, he congratulated himself that his gamble had paid off. He hadn't risen to senior rank in the Secret Service by dwelling on what might have been. This kind of work ran in the family. The girl was obviously a natural.

'No, I don't think so. I don't like to waste human resources. Leave her file open.'

Glossary of terms

Asante – thank you

Asante sana – thank you very much

Hakuna matata – no worries

Habari – how are you?

Jambo – hello

Kali – bad

Kali sana – very bad

Karibu – welcome

Mandazis – small fried buns

Matatus – bus taxi

Mzungu – white person

Mzuri – good

Pole sana – very sorry

Safari mzuri – good travels

Sawa – (or sasa) OK

Coming Soon . .